Hershberger

Mother Goose in Prose

"There was a little man and he had a little gun"

MOTHER GOOSE IN PROSE

BY L. FRANK BAUM

Illustrated by MAXFIELD PARRISH

BOUNTY BOOKS
NEW YORK

Library of Congress Catalog Card Number: 74-19434

This edition is published by Bounty Books
a division of Crown Publishers, Inc.
a b c d e f g h
Manufactured in the United States of America

Contents

Illustrations

Introduction.

Introduction

NONE of us, whether children or adults, needs an introduction to Mother Goose. Those things which are earliest impressed upon our minds cling to them the most tenaciously. The snatches sung in the nursery are never forgotten, nor are they ever recalled without bringing back with them myriads of slumbering feelings and half-forgotten images.

We hear the sweet, low voice of the mother, singing soft lullabies to her darling, and see the kindly, wrinkled face of the grandmother as she croons the old ditties to quiet our restless spirits. One generation is linked to another by the everlasting spirit of song; the ballads of the nursery follow us from childhood to old age, and they are readily brought from memory's recesses at any time to amuse our children or our grandchildren.

The collection of jingles we know and love as the "Melodies of Mother Goose" are evidently drawn from a variety of sources. While they are, taken altogether, a happy union of rhyme, wit, pathos, satire and sentiment, the research after the author of each individual verse would indeed be hopeless. It would be folly to suppose them all the composition of uneducated old nurses, for many of them contain much reflection, wit and melody. It is said that Shelley wrote "Pussy-Cat Mew," and Dean Swift "Little Bo-Peep," and these assertions are as difficult to disprove as to prove. Some of the older verses, however, are doubtless offshoots from ancient Folk Lore songs, and have descended to us through many centuries.

The connection of Mother Goose with the rhymes which bear her name is difficult to determine, and, in fact, three countries claim her for their own: France, England and America.

About the year 1650 there appeared in circulation in London a small book, named "Rhymes of the Nursery; or Lulla-Byes for Children," which contained many of the identical pieces that have been handed down to us; but the name of Mother Goose was evidently not then known. In this edition were the rhymes of "Little Jack Horner," "Old King Cole," "Mistress Mary," "Sing a Song o' Sixpence," and "Little Boy Blue."

In 1697 Charles Perrault published in France a book of children's tales entitled "Contes de ma Mére Oye," and this is really the first time we find authentic record of the use of the name of Mother Goose, although Perrault's tales differ materially from those we now know under this title. They comprised "The Sleeping Beauty," "The Fairy," "Little Red Riding-Hood," "Blue Beard," "Puss in Boots," "Riquet with the Tuft," "Cinderella," and "Little Thumb;" eight stories in all. On the cover of the book was depicted an old lady holding in her hand a distaff and surrounded by a group of children listening eagerly. Mr. Andrew Lang has edited a beautiful English edition of this work (Oxford, 1888).

America bases her claim to Mother Goose upon the following statement, made by the late John Fleet Eliot, a descendant of Thomas Fleet, the printer:

At the beginning of the eighteenth century there lived in Boston a lady named Eliza Goose (written also Vergoose and Vertigoose) who belonged to a wealthy family. Her eldest daughter, Elizabeth Goose (or Vertigoose), was married by Rev. Cotton Mather in 1715 to an enterprising and industrious printer named Thomas Fleet, and in due time gave birth to a son. Like most mothers-in-law in our day, the importance of Mrs. Goose increased with the appearance of her grandchild, and poor Mr. Fleet, half distracted with her endless nursery ditties, finding all other means fail, tried what ridicule could effect, and actually printed a book under the title "Songs of the Nursery; or, Mother Goose's Melodies for Children." On the title page was the picture of a goose with a very long neck and a mouth wide open, and below this, "Printed by T. Fleet, at his Printing House in Pudding Lane, 1719. Price, two coppers."

Mr. Wm. A. Wheeler, the editor of Hurd & Houghton's elaborate edition of Mother Goose, (1870), reiterated this assertion, and a writer in the Boston Transcript of June 17, 1864, says: "Fleet's book was partly a reprint of an English collection of songs, (Barclay's), and the new title was doubtless a compliment by the printer to his mother-in-law Goose for her contributions. She was the mother of sixteen children and a typical 'Old Woman who lived in a Shoe.'"

We may take it to be true that Fleet's wife was of the Vergoose family, and that the name was often contracted to Goose. But the rest of the story is unsupported by any evidence whatever. In fact, all that Mr. Eliot knew of it was the statement of the late Edward A. Crowninshield, of Boston, that he had seen Fleet's edition in the library of the American Antiquarian Society. Repeated researches at Worcester having failed to bring to light this supposed copy, and no record of it appearing on any catalogue there, we may dismiss the entire story with the supposition that Mr. Eliot misunderstood the remarks made to him. Indeed, as Mr. William H. Whitmore points out in his clever monograph upon Mother Goose (Albany, 1889), it is very doubtful whether in 1719 a Boston printer would have been allowed to publish such "trivial" rhymes. "Boston children at that date," says Mr. Whitmore, "were fed upon Gospel food, and it seems extremely improbable that an edition could have been sold."

Singularly enough, England's claim to the venerable old lady is of about the same date as Boston's. There lived in a town in Sussex, about the year 1704, an old woman named Martha Gooch. She was a capital nurse, and in great demand to care for newly-born babies; therefore, through long years of service as nurse, she came to be called Mother Gooch. This good woman had one peculiarity: she was accustomed to croon queer rhymes and jingles over the cradles of her charges, and these rhymes "seemed so senseless and silly to the people who overheard them" that they began to call her "Mother Goose," in derision, the term being derived from Queen Goosefoot, the mother of Charlemagne. The old nurse paid no attention to her critics, but continued to sing her rhymes as before; for, however much grown people might laugh at her, the children seemed to enjoy them very much, and not one of them was too peevish to be quieted and soothed by her verses. At one time Mistress Gooch was nursing a child of Mr. Ronald Barclay, a physician residing in the town, and he noticed the rhymes she sang and became interested in them. In time he wrote them all down and made a book of them, which it is said was printed by John Worthington & Son in the Strand, London, in 1712, under the name of "Ye Melodious Rhymes of Mother Goose." But even this story of Martha Gooch is based upon very meager and unsatisfactory evidence.

The earliest English edition of Mother Goose's Melodies that is absolutely authentic was issued by

John Newbury of London about the year 1760, and the first authentic American edition was a reprint of Newbury's made by Isaiah Thomas of Worcester, Mass., in 1785.

None of the earlier editions, however, contained all the rhymes so well known at the present day, since every decade has added its quota to the mass of jingles attributed to "Mother Goose." Some of the earlier verses have become entirely obsolete, and it is well they have, for many were crude and silly and others were coarse. It is simply a result of the greater refinement of modern civilization that they have been relegated to oblivion, while the real gems of the collection will doubtless live and grow in popular favor for many ages.

While I have taken some pains to record the various claims to the origin of Mother Goose, it does not matter in the least whether she was in reality a myth, or a living Eliza Goose, Martha Gooch or the "Mére Oye" of Perrault. The songs that cluster around her name are what we love, and each individual verse appeals more to the childish mind than does Mother Goose herself.

Many of these nursery rhymes are complete tales in themselves, telling their story tersely but completely; there are others which are but bare suggestions, leaving the imagination to weave in the details of the story. Perhaps therein may lie part of their charm, but however that may be I have thought the children might like the stories told at greater length, that they may dwell the longer upon their favorite heroes and heroines.

For that reason I have written this book.

In making the stories I have followed mainly the suggestions of the rhymes, and my hope is that the little ones will like them, and not find that they interfere with the fanciful creations of their own imaginations.

L. FRANK BAUM.

Chicago, Illinois, July, 1899.

Sing a Song o' Sixpence

Sing a Song o' Sixpence

Sing a song o' sixpence, a handful of rye,
Four-and-twenty blackbirds baked in a pie;
When the pie was opened the birds began to sing,
Was n't that a dainty dish to set before the King?

Sing a Song o' Sixpence

IF you have never heard the legend of Gilligren and the King's pie you will scarcely understand the above verse; so I will tell you the whole story, and then you will be able to better appreciate the rhyme.

Gilligren was an orphan, and lived with an uncle and aunt who were very unkind to him. They cuffed him and scolded him upon the slightest provocation, and made his life very miserable indeed. Gilligren never rebelled against this treatment, but bore their cruelty silently and with patience, although often he longed to leave them and seek a home amongst kinder people.

It so happened that when Gilligren was twelve years old the King died, and his son was to be proclaimed King in his place, and crowned with great ceremony. People were flocking to London from all parts of the country, to witness the festivities, and the boy longed to go with them.

One evening he said to his uncle,

"If I had sixpence I could make my fortune."

"Pooh! nonsense!" exclaimed his uncle, "a sixpence is a small thing. How then could you make a fortune from it?"

"That I cannot tell you," replied Gilligren, "but if you will give me the sixpence I will go to London, and not return until I am a rich man."

"The boy is a fool!" said his uncle, with anger; but the aunt spoke up quickly.

"Give him the money and let him go," she said, "and then we shall be well rid of him and no longer be obliged to feed and clothe him at our expense."

"Well," said her husband, after a moment's thought, "here is the money; but remember, this is all I shall ever give you, and when it is gone you must not come to me for more."

"Never fear," replied Gilligren, joyfully, as he put the sixpence in his pocket, "I shall not trouble you again."

The next morning he cut a short stick to assist him in walking, and after bidding good-bye to his uncle and aunt he started upon his journey to London.

"The money will not last him two days," said the man, as he watched Gilligren go down the turnpike road, "and when it is gone he will starve to death."

"Or he may fall in with people who will treat him worse than we did," rejoined the woman, "and then he 'll wish he had never left us."

But Gilligren, nothing dismayed by thoughts of the future, trudged bravely along the London road. The world was before him, and the bright sunshine glorified the dusty road and lightened the tips of the dark green hedges that bordered his path. At the end of his pilgrimage was the great city, and he never doubted he would find therein proper work and proper pay, and much better treatment than he was accustomed to receive.

So, on he went, whistling merrily to while away the time, watching the sparrows skim over the fields, and enjoying to the full the unusual sights that met his eyes. At noon he overtook a carter, who divided with the boy his luncheon of bread and cheese, and for supper a farmer's wife gave him a bowl of milk. When it grew dark he crawled under a hedge and slept soundly until dawn.

The next day he kept steadily upon his way, and toward evening met a farmer with a wagon loaded with sacks of grain.

"Where are you going, my lad?" asked the man.

"To London," replied Gilligren, "to see the King crowned."

"Have you any money?" enquired the farmer.

"Oh yes," answered Gilligren, "I have a sixpence."

"If you will give me the sixpence," said the man, "I will give you a sack of rye for it."

"What could I do with a sack of rye?" asked Gilligren, wonderingly.

"Take it to the mill, and get it ground into flour. With the flour you could have bread baked, and that you can sell."

"That is a good idea," replied Gilligren, "so here is my sixpence, and now give me the sack of rye."

The farmer put the sixpence carefully into his pocket, and then reached under the seat of the wagon and drew out a sack, which he cast on the ground at the boy's feet.

"There is your sack of rye," he said, with a laugh.

"But the sack is empty!" remonstrated Gilligren.

"Oh, no; there is some rye in it."

"But only a handful!" said Gilligren, when he had opened the mouth of the sack and gazed within it.

"It is a sack of rye, nevertheless," replied the wicked farmer, "and I did not say how much rye there would be in the sack I would give you. Let this be a lesson to you never again to buy grain without looking into the sack!" and with that he whipped up his horses and left Gilligren standing in the road with the sack at his feet and nearly ready to cry at his loss.

"My sixpence is gone," he said to himself, "and I have received nothing in exchange but a handful of rye! How can I make my fortune with that?"

He did not despair, however, but picked up the sack and continued his way along the dusty road. Soon it became too dark to travel farther, and Gilligren stepped aside into a meadow, where, lying down upon the sweet grass, he rolled the sack into a pillow for his head and prepared to sleep.

The rye that was within the sack, however, hurt his head, and he sat up and opened the sack.

"Why should I keep a handful of rye?" he thought, "It will be of no value to me at all."

So he threw out the rye upon the ground, and rolling up the sack again for a pillow, was soon sound asleep.

When he awoke the sun was shining brightly over his head and the twitter and chirping of many birds fell upon his ears. Gilligren opened his eyes and saw a large flock of blackbirds feeding upon the rye he had scattered upon the ground. So intent were they upon their feast they never noticed Gilligren at all.

He carefully unfolded the sack, and spreading wide its opening threw it quickly over the flock of blackbirds. Some escaped and flew away, but a great many were caught, and Gilligren put his eye to the sack and found he had captured four and twenty. He tied the mouth of the sack with a piece of twine that was in his pocket, and then threw the sack over his shoulder and began again his journey to London.

"I have made a good exchange, after all," he thought, "for surely four and twenty blackbirds are worth more than a handful of rye, and perhaps even more than a sixpence, if I can find anyone who wishes to buy them."

He now walked rapidly forward, and about noon entered the great city of London.

Gilligren wandered about the streets until he came to the King's palace, where there was a great concourse of people and many guards to keep intruders from the gates.

Seeing he could not enter from the front, the boy walked around to the rear of the palace and found himself near the royal kitchen, where the cooks and other servants were rushing around to hasten the preparation of the King's dinner.

Gilligren sat down upon a stone where he could watch them, and laying the sack at his feet was soon deeply interested in the strange sight.

Presently a servant in the King's livery saw him and came to his side.

"What are you doing here?" he asked, roughly.

"I am waiting to see the King," replied Gilligren.

"The King! The King never comes here," said the servant; "and neither do we allow idlers about the royal kitchen. So depart at once, or I shall be forced to call a guard to arrest you."

Gilligren arose obediently and slung his sack over his shoulder. As he did so the birds that were within began to flutter.

"What have you in the sack?" asked the servant.

"Blackbirds," replied Gilligren.

"Blackbirds!" echoed the servant, in surprise,

"well, that is very fortunate indeed. Come with me at once!" He seized the boy by the arm and drew him hastily along until they entered the great kitchen of the palace.

"Here, Mister Baker!" the man called, excitedly, "I have found your blackbirds!"

A big, fat man who was standing in the middle of the kitchen with folded arms and a look of despair upon his round, greasy face, at once came toward them and asked eagerly,

"The blackbirds? are you sure you can get them?"

"They are here already; the boy has a bag full of them."

"Give them to me," said the cook, who wore a square cap, that was shaped like a box, upon his head.

"What do you want with them?" asked Gilligren.

"I want them for a pie for the King's dinner," answered Mister Baker; "His Majesty ordered the dish, and I have hunted all over London for the blackbirds, but could not find them. Now that you have brought them, however, you have saved me my position as cook, and perhaps my head as well."

"But it would be cruel to put the beautiful birds in a pie," remonstrated Gilligren, "and I shall not give them to you for such a purpose."

"Nonsense!" replied the cook, "the King has ordered it; he is very fond of the dish."

"Still, you cannot have them," declared the boy

stoutly, "the birds are mine, and I will not have them killed."

"But what can I do?" asked the cook, in perplexity; "the King has ordered a blackbird pie, and your birds are the only blackbirds in London."

Gilligren thought deeply for a moment, and conceived what he thought to be a very good idea. If the sixpence was to make his fortune, then this was his great opportunity.

"You can have the blackbirds on two conditions," he said.

"What are they?" asked the cook.

"One is that you will not kill the birds. The other condition is that you secure me a position in the King's household."

"How can I put live birds in a pie?" enquired the cook.

"Very easily, if you make the pie big enough to hold them. You can serve the pie after the King has satisfied his hunger with other dishes, and it will amuse the company to find live birds in the pie when they expected cooked ones."

"It is a risky experiment," exclaimed the cook, "for I do not know the new King's temper. But the idea may please His Majesty, and since you will not allow me to kill the birds, it is the best thing I can do. As for your other condition, you seem to be a very bright boy, and so I will have the butler take you as his page, and you shall stand back of the King's chair and keep the flies away while he eats."

The butler being called, and his consent secured, the cook fell to making the crusts for his novel pie, while Gilligren was taken to the servants' hall and dressed in a gorgeous suit of the King's livery.

When the dinner was served, the King kept looking for the blackbird pie, but he said nothing, and at last the pie was placed before him, its crusts looking light and brown, and sprigs of myrtle being stuck in the four corners to make it look more inviting.

Although the King had already eaten heartily, he smacked his lips when he saw this tempting dish, and picking up the carving-fork he pushed it quickly into the pie.

At once the crust fell in, and all the four and twenty blackbirds put up their heads and began to look about them. And coming from the blackness of the pie into the brilliantly lighted room they thought they were in the sunshine, and began to sing merrily, while some of the boldest hopped out upon the table or began flying around the room.

At first the good King was greatly surprised; but soon, appreciating the jest, he lay back in his chair and laughed long and merrily. And his courtiers and the fine ladies present heartily joined in the laughter, for they also were greatly amused.

Then the King called for the cook, and when

Mister Baker appeared, uncertain of his reception, and filled with many misgivings, His Majesty cried,

"Sirrah! how came you to think of putting live birds in the pie?"

The cook, fearing that the King was angry, answered,

"May it please your Majesty, it was not my thought, but the idea of the boy who stands behind your chair."

The King turned his head, and seeing Gilligren, who looked very well in his new livery, he said,

"You are a clever youth, and deserve a better position than that of a butler's lad. Hereafter you shall be one of my own pages, and if you serve me faithfully I will advance your fortunes with your deserts."

And Gilligren did serve the King faithfully, and as he grew older acquired much honor and great wealth.

"After all," he used to say, "that sixpence made my fortune. And it all came about through such a small thing as a handful of rye!"

The Story of
Little Boy Blue

The Story of Little Boy Blue

Little Boy Blue, come blow your horn,
The sheep 's in the meadow, the cow 's in the corn;
Where 's the little boy that minds the sheep?
He 's under the haystack, fast asleep!

THERE once lived a poor widow who supported herself and her only son by gleaning in the fields the stalks of grain that had been missed by the reapers. Her little cottage was at the foot of a beautiful valley, upon the edge of the river that wound in and out among the green hills; and although poor, she was contented with her lot, for her home was pleasant and her lovely boy was a constant delight to her.

He had big blue eyes, and fair golden curls, and he loved his good mother very dearly, and was never more pleased than when she allowed him to help her with her work.

And so the years passed happily away till the boy was eight years old, but then the widow fell sick, and their little store of money melted gradually away.

"I do n't know what we shall do for bread," she said, kissing her boy with tears in her eyes, "for I am not yet strong enough to work, and we have no money left."

"But I can work," answered the boy; "and I'm sure if I go to the Squire up at the Hall he will give me something to do."

At first the widow was reluctant to consent to this, since she loved to keep her child at her side, but finally, as nothing else could be done, she decided to let him go to see the Squire.

Being too proud to allow her son to go to the great house in his ragged clothes, she made him a new suit out of a pretty blue dress she had herself worn in happier times, and when it was finished and the boy dressed in it, he looked as pretty as a prince in a fairy tale. For the bright blue jacket set off his curls to good advantage, and the color just matched the blue of his eyes. His trousers were blue, also, and she took the silver buckles from her own shoes and put them on his, that he might appear the finer. And then she brushed his curls and placed his big straw hat upon them and sent him away with a kiss to see the Squire.

It so happened that the great man was walking in his garden with his daughter Madge that morning, and was feeling in an especially happy mood, so that when he suddenly looked up and saw a little boy before him, he said, kindly,

"Well, my child, what can I do for you?"

"If you please, sir," said the boy, bravely, although he was frightened at meeting the Squire face to face, "I want you to give me some work to do, so that I can earn money."

"Earn money!" repeated the Squire, "why do you wish to earn money?"

"To buy food for my mother, sir. We are very poor, and since she is no longer able to work for me I wish to work for her."

"But what can you do?" asked the Squire; "you are too small to work in the fields."

"I could earn something, sir, could n't I?"

His tone was so pleading that mistress Madge was unable to resist it, and even the Squire was touched. The young lady came forward and took the boy's hand in her own, and pressing back his curls, she kissed his fair cheek.

"You shall be our shepherd," she said, pleasantly, "and keep the sheep out of the meadows and the cows from getting into the corn. You know, father," she continued, turning to the Squire, "it was only yesterday you said you must get a boy to tend the sheep, and this little boy can do it nicely."

"Very well," replied the Squire, "it shall be as you say, and if he is attentive and watchful he will be able to save me a good bit of trouble and so really earn his money."

Then he turned to the child and said,

"Come to me in the morning, my little man, and I will give you a silver horn to blow, that you may call the sheep and the cows whenever they go astray. What is your name?"

"Oh, never mind his name, papa!" broke in the

Squire's daughter; "I shall call him Little Boy Blue, since he is dressed in blue from head to foot, and his dress but matches his eyes. And you must give him a good wage, also, for surely no Squire before ever had a prettier shepherd boy than this."

"Very good," said the Squire, cheerfully, as he pinched his daughter's rosy cheek; "be watchful, Little Boy Blue, and you shall be well paid."

Then Little Boy Blue thanked them both very sweetly and ran back over the hill and into the valley where his home lay nestled by the river-side, to tell the good news to his mother.

The poor widow wept tears of joy when she heard his story, and smiled when he told her that his name was to be Little Boy Blue. She knew the Squire was a kind master and would be good to her darling son.

Early the next morning Little Boy Blue was at the Hall, and the Squire's steward gave him a new silver horn, that glistened brightly in the sunshine, and a golden cord to fasten it around his neck. And then he was given charge of the sheep and the cows, and told to keep them from straying into the meadow-lands and the fields of grain.

It was not hard work, but just suited to Little Boy Blue's age, and he was watchful and vigilant and made a very good shepherd boy indeed. His mother needed food no longer, for the Squire paid her son liberally and the Squire's daughter made a favorite of the small shepherd and loved to hear the call of his silver horn echoing amongst the hills. Even the sheep and the cows were fond of him, and always obeyed the sound of his horn; therefore the Squire's corn thrived finely, and was never trampled.

Little Boy Blue was now very happy, and his mother was proud and contented and began to improve in health. After a few weeks she became strong enough to leave the cottage and walk a little in the fields each day; but she could not go far, because her limbs were too feeble to support her long, so the most she could attempt was to walk as far as the stile to meet Little Boy Blue as he came home from work in the evening. Then she would lean on his shoulder and return to the cottage with him, and the boy was very glad he could thus support his darling mother and assist her faltering steps.

But one day a great misfortune came upon them, since it is true that no life can be so happy but that sorrow will creep in to temper it.

Little Boy Blue came homeward one evening very light of heart and whistled merrily as he walked, for he thought he should find his mother awaiting him at the stile and a good supper spread upon the table in the little cottage. But when he came to the stile his mother was not in sight, and in answer to his call a low moan of pain reached his ears.

Little Boy Blue sprang over the stile and found lying upon the ground his dear mother, her face white and drawn with suffering, and tears of anguish running down her cheeks. For she had slipped upon the stile and fallen, and her leg was broken!

Little Boy Blue ran to the cottage for water and bathed the poor woman's face, and raised her head that she might drink. There were no neighbors, for the cottage stood all alone by the river, so the child was obliged to support his mother in his arms as best he could while she crawled painfully back to the cottage. Fortunately, it was not far, and at last she was safely laid upon her bed. Then Little Boy Blue began to think what he should do next.

"Can I leave you alone while I go for the doctor, mamma?" he asked, anxiously, as he held her clasped hands tightly in his two little ones. His mother drew him towards her and kissed him.

"Take the boat, dear," she said, "and fetch the doctor from the village. I shall be patient till you return."

Little Boy Blue rushed away to the river bank and unfastened the little boat; and then he pulled sturdily down the river until he passed the bend and came to the pretty village below. When he had found the doctor and told of his mother's misfortune, the good man promised to attend him at once, and very soon they were seated in the boat and on their way to the cottage.

It was very dark by this time, but Little Boy Blue knew every turn and bend in the river, and the doctor helped him pull at the oars, so that at last they came

Little Boy Blue

to the place where a faint light twinkled through the cottage window. They found the poor woman in much pain, but the doctor quickly set and bandaged her leg, and gave her some medicine to ease her suffering. It was nearly midnight when all was finished and the doctor was ready to start back to the village.

"Take good care of your mother," he said to the boy, "and do n't worry about her, for it is not a bad break and the leg will mend nicely in time; but she will be in bed many days, and you must nurse her as well as you are able."

All through the night the boy sat by the bedside, bathing his mother's fevered brow and ministering to her wants. And when the day broke she was resting easily and the pain had left her, and she told Little Boy Blue he must go to his work.

"For," said she, "more than ever now we need the money you earn from the Squire, as my misfortune will add to the expenses of living, and we have the doctor to pay. Do not fear to leave me, for I shall rest quietly and sleep most of the time while you are away."

Little Boy Blue did not like to leave his mother all alone, but he knew of no one he could ask to stay with her; so he placed food and water by her bedside, and ate a little breakfast himself, and started off to tend his sheep.

The sun was shining brightly, and the birds sang sweetly in the trees, and the crickets chirped just as merrily as if this great trouble had not come to Little Boy Blue to make him sad.

But he went bravely to his work, and for several hours he watched carefully; and the men at work in the fields, and the Squire's daughter, who sat embroidering upon the porch of the great house, heard often the sound of his horn as he called the straying sheep to his side.

But he had not slept the whole night, and he was tired with his long watch at his mother's bedside, and so in spite of himself the lashes would droop occasionally over his blue eyes, for he was only a child, and children feel the loss of sleep more than older people.

Still, Little Boy Blue had no intention of sleeping while he was on duty, and bravely fought against the drowsiness that was creeping over him. The sun shone very hot that day, and he walked to the shady side of a big haystack and sat down upon the ground, leaning his back against the stack.

The cows and sheep were quietly browsing near him, and he watched them earnestly for a time, listening to the singing of the birds, and the gentle tinkling of the bells upon the wethers, and the far-away songs of the reapers that the breeze brought to his ears. And before he knew it the blue eyes had closed fast, and the golden head lay back upon the hay, and Little Boy Blue was fast asleep and dreaming that his mother was well again and had come to the stile to meet him.

The sheep strayed near the edge of the meadow and paused, waiting for the warning sound of the horn. And the breeze carried the fragrance of the growing corn to the nostrils of the browsing cows and tempted them nearer and nearer to the forbidden feast. But the silver horn was silent, and before long the cows were feeding upon the Squire's pet cornfield and the sheep were enjoying themselves amidst the juicy grasses of the meadows.

The Squire himself was returning from a long, weary ride over his farms, and when he came to the cornfield and saw the cows trampling down the grain and feeding upon the golden stalks he was very angry.

"Little Boy Blue!" he cried; "ho! Little Boy Blue, come blow your horn!" But there was no reply. He rode on a way and now discovered that the sheep were deep within the meadows, and that made him more angry still.

"Here, Isaac," he said to a farmer's lad who chanced to pass by, "where is Little Boy Blue?"

"He 's under the hay-stack, your honor, fast asleep!" replied Isaac with a grin, for he had passed that way and seen that the boy was lying asleep.

"Will you go and wake him?" asked the Squire; "for he must drive out the sheep and the cows before they do more damage."

"Not I," replied Isaac, "if I wake him he 'll surely cry, for he is but a baby, and not fit to mind the sheep. But I myself will drive them out for your honor," and away he ran to do so, thinking that now the Squire would give him Little Boy Blue's place, and make him the shepherd boy, for Isaac had long coveted the position.

The Squire's daughter, hearing the angry tones of her father's voice, now came out to see what was amiss, and when she heard that Little Boy Blue had failed in his trust she was deeply grieved, for she had loved the child for his pretty ways.

The Squire dismounted from his horse and came to where the boy was lying.

"Awake!" said he, shaking him by the shoulder, "and depart from my lands, for you have betrayed my trust, and let the sheep and the cows stray into the fields and meadows!"

Little Boy Blue started up at once and rubbed his eyes; and then he did as Isaac prophesied, and began to weep bitterly, for his heart was sore that he had failed in his duty to the good Squire and so forfeited his confidence.

But the Squire's daughter was moved by the child's tears, so she took him upon her lap and comforted him, asking,

"Why did you sleep, Little Boy Blue, when you should have watched the cows and the sheep?"

"My mother has broken her leg," answered the boy, between his sobs, "and I did not sleep all last night, but sat by her bedside nursing her. And I tried hard not to fall asleep, but could not help myself;

and oh, Squire! I hope you will forgive me this once, for my poor mother's sake!"

"Where does your mother live?" asked the Squire, in a kindly tone, for he had already forgiven Little Boy Blue.

"In the cottage down by the river," answered the child; "and she is all alone, for there is no one near to help us in our trouble."

"Come," said Mistress Madge, rising to her feet and taking his hand; "lead us to your home, and we will see if we cannot assist your poor mother."

So the Squire and his daughter and Little Boy Blue all walked down to the little cottage, and the Squire had a long talk with the poor widow. And that same day a big basket of dainties was sent to the cottage, and Mistress Madge bade her own maid go to the widow and nurse her carefully until she recovered.

So that after all Little Boy Blue did more for his dear mother by falling asleep than he could had he kept wide awake; for after his mother was well again the Squire gave them a pretty cottage to live in very near to the great house itself, and the Squire's daughter was ever afterward their good friend, and saw that they wanted for no comforts of life.

And Little Boy Blue did not fall asleep again at his post, but watched the cows and the sheep faithfully for many years, until he grew up to manhood and had a farm of his own.

He always said his mother's accident had brought him good luck, but I think it was rather his own loving heart and his devotion to his mother that made him friends. For no one is afraid to trust a boy who loves to serve and care for his mother.

The Cat and the Fiddle

The Cat and the Fiddle

Hey, diddle, diddle,
The cat and the fiddle,
The cow jumped over the moon!
The little dog laughed
To see such sport,
And the dish ran off with the spoon!

PERHAPS you think this verse is all nonsense, and that the things it mentions could never have happened; but they did happen, as you will understand when I have explained them all to you clearly.

Little Bobby was the only son of a small farmer who lived out of town upon a country road. Bobby's mother looked after the house and Bobby's father took care of the farm, and Bobby himself, who was not very big, helped them both as much as he was able.

It was lonely upon the farm, especially when his father and mother were both busy at work, but the boy had one way to amuse himself that served to pass many an hour when he would not otherwise have known what to do. He was very fond of music, and his father one day brought him from the town a small fiddle, or violin, which he soon learned to play upon. I don't suppose he was a very fine musician, but the tunes he played pleased himself, as well as his father and mother, and Bobby's fiddle soon became his constant companion.

One day in the warm summer the farmer and his wife determined to drive to the town to sell their butter and eggs and bring back some groceries in exchange for them, and while they were gone Bobby was to be left alone.

"We shall not be back till late in the evening," said his mother, "for the weather is too warm to drive very fast. But I have left you a dish of bread and milk for your supper, and you must be a good boy and amuse yourself with your fiddle until we return."

Bobby promised to be good and look after the house, and then his father and mother climbed into the wagon and drove away to the town.

The boy was not entirely alone, for there was the big black tabby-cat lying upon the floor in the kitchen, and the little yellow dog barking at the wagon as it drove away, and the big moolie-cow lowing in the pasture down by the brook. Animals are often very good company, and Bobby did not feel nearly as lonely as he would had there been no living thing about the house.

Besides he had some work to do in the garden, pulling up the weeds that grew thick in the carrot-bed, and when the last faint sounds of the wheels had died away he went into the garden and began his task.

The little dog went too, for dogs love to be with

people and to watch what is going on; and he sat down near Bobby and cocked up his ears and wagged his tail and seemed to take a great interest in the weeding. Once in a while he would rush away to chase a butterfly or bark at a beetle that crawled through the garden, but he always came back to the boy and kept near his side.

By and by the cat, which found it lonely in the big, empty kitchen, now that Bobby's mother was gone, came walking into the garden also, and lay down upon a path in the sunshine and lazily watched the boy at his work. The dog and the cat were good friends, having lived together so long that they did not care to fight each other. To be sure Towser, as the little dog was called, sometimes tried to tease pussy, being himself very mischievous; but when the cat put out her sharp claws and showed her teeth, Towser, like a wise little dog, quickly ran away, and so they managed to get along in a friendly manner.

By the time the carrot-bed was all weeded, the sun was sinking behind the edge of the forest and the new moon rising in the east, and now Bobby began to feel hungry and went into the house for his dish of bread and milk.

"I think I'll take my supper down to the brook," he said to himself, "and sit upon the grassy bank while I eat it. And I'll take my fiddle, too, and play upon it to pass the time until father and mother come home."

It was a good idea, for down by the brook it was cool and pleasant; so Bobby took his fiddle under his arm and carried his dish of bread and milk down to the bank that sloped to the edge of the brook. It was rather a steep bank, but Bobby sat upon the edge, and placing his fiddle beside him, leaned against a tree and began to eat his supper.

The little dog had followed at his heels, and the cat also came slowly walking after him, and as Bobby ate, they sat one on either side of him and looked earnestly into his face as if they too were hungry. So he threw some of the bread to Towser, who grabbed it eagerly and swallowed it in the twinkling of an eye. And Bobby left some of the milk in the dish for the cat, also, and she came lazily up and drank it in a dainty, sober fashion, and licked both the dish and spoon until no drop of the milk was left.

Then Bobby picked up his fiddle and tuned it and began to play some of the pretty tunes he knew. And while he played he watched the moon rise higher and higher until it was reflected in the smooth, still water of the brook. Indeed, Bobby could not tell which was the plainest to see, the moon in the sky or the moon in the water. The little dog lay quietly on one side of him, and the cat softly purred upon the other, and even the moolie-cow was attracted by the music and wandered near until she was browsing the grass at the edge of the brook.

After a time, when Bobby had played all the tunes

he knew, he laid the fiddle down beside him, near to where the cat slept, and then he lay down upon the bank and began to think.

It is very hard to think long upon a dreamy summer night without falling asleep, and very soon Bobby's eyes closed and he forgot all about the dog and the cat and the cow and the fiddle, and dreamed he was Jack the Giant Killer and was just about to slay the biggest giant in the world.

And while he dreamed, the cat sat up and yawned and stretched herself, and then began wagging her long tail from side to side and watching the moon that was reflected in the water.

But the fiddle lay just behind her, and as she moved her tail, she drew it between the strings of the fiddle, where it caught fast. Then she gave her tail a jerk and pulled the fiddle against the tree, which made a loud noise. This frightened the cat greatly, and not knowing what was the matter with her tail, she started to run as fast as she could. But still the fiddle clung to her tail, and at every step it bounded along and made such a noise that she screamed with terror. And in her fright she ran straight towards the cow, which, seeing a black streak coming at her, and hearing the racket made by the fiddle, became also frightened and made such a jump to get out of the way that she jumped right across the brook, leaping over the very spot where the moon shone in the water!

Bobby had been awakened by the noise, and opened his eyes in time to see the cow jump; and at first it seemed to him that she had actually jumped over the moon in the sky, instead of the one in the brook.

The dog was delighted at the sudden excitement caused by the cat, and ran barking and dancing along the bank, so that he presently knocked against the dish, and behold! it slid down the bank, carrying the spoon with it, and fell with a splash into the water of the brook.

As soon as Bobby recovered from his surprise he ran after the cat, which had raced to the house, and soon came to where the fiddle lay upon the ground, it having at last dropped from the cat's tail. He examined it carefully, and was glad to find it was not hurt, in spite of its rough usage. And then he had to go across the brook and drive the cow back over the little bridge, and also to roll up his sleeve and reach into the water to recover the dish and the spoon.

Then he went back to the house and lighted a lamp, and sat down to compose a new tune before his father and mother returned.

The cat had recovered from her fright and lay quietly under the stove, and Towser sat upon the floor panting, with his mouth wide open, and looking so comical that Bobby thought he was actually laughing at the whole occurrence.

The Cat and the Fiddle

And these were the words to the tune that Bobby composed that night:

Hey, diddle, diddle,
The cat and the fiddle,
The cow jumped over the moon!
The little dog laughed
To see such sport,
And the dish ran away with the spoon!

The Black Sheep

The Black Sheep

Black sheep, black sheep, have you any wool?
Yes, my little master, three bags full;
One for my master and one for his dame,
And one for the little boy that lives in the lane.

IT was a bright spring day, and the sun shone very warm and pleasant over the pastures, where the new grass was growing so juicy and tender that all the sheep thought they had never tasted anything so delicious.

The sheep had had a strange experience that morning, for the farmer had taken them down to the brook and washed them, and then he tied their legs together and laid them on the grass and clipped all the heavy, soft wool from their bodies with a great pair of shears.

The sheep did not like this very well, for every once in a while the shears would pull the wool and hurt them; and when they were sheared they felt very strange, for it was almost as if someone took off all your clothes and let you run around naked. None of them were in a very good temper this morning, although the sun shone so warmly and the grass was so sweet, and as they watched the farmer and his man carry their wool up to the house in great bags, the old ram said, crossly,

"I hope they are satisfied, now that they have stolen from us all our soft, warm fleece."

"What are they going to do with it?" asked one of the sheep.

"Oh, they will spin it into threads and make coats for the men and dresses for the women. For men are such strange creatures that no wool grows on them at all, and that is why they selfishly rob us of our fleece that they may cover their own skinny bodies!"

"It must be horrid to be a man," said the Black Sheep, "and not to have any wool grow on you at all. I'm sorry for that little boy that lives in the lane, for he will never be able to keep warm unless we give him some of our wool."

"But what a shame it is," continued the ram, "for the farmer to steal all the wool from us when we have taken all the trouble to grow it!"

"I don't mind," bleated a young lamb named Frisky, as it kicked up its heels and gambolled about upon the grass; "it's nice to have all that heavy wool cut off my back, for I sha'n't have to carry it around wherever I go."

"Oh, indeed!" sneered the ram, "you like it, do you? Have you any idea what you look like, all sheared down to your skin? How would you like to have someone come along and see you, now that you are all head and legs?"

"Oh, I would n't mind," said the lamb again; "I shall grow more wool by winter-time, and I 'm sure I do n't look any worse than you do."

Some of the sheep looked at the ram and began to titter, for he was old and thin, and looked very comical indeed without any wool. And this made him so angry that he went off by himself and began eating grass, and would not speak to the others at all.

"I do n't know why sheep should feel badly about having their fleeces cut," remarked the Black Sheep, thoughtfully, "for the farmer is very kind to us, and so is his dame, and I am glad my wool serves to keep them warm in the winter. For before the snow comes our wool will grow out again, and we shall not be any the worse for our loss."

"What do those people who have n't any sheep do for clothes?" asked the lamb.

"I 'm sure I do n't know. They must nearly freeze in the winter. Perhaps the ram can tell us."

But the ram was still angry, and refused to say anything, so the sheep stopped talking and began to scatter over the pasture and eat the tender, new grass.

By and by the Black Sheep wandered near the lane, and looking up, saw the little boy watching it through the bars.

"Good morning, Black Sheep," said the boy; "why do you look so funny this morning?"

"They have cut off my wool," answered the sheep.

"What will they do with it, Black Sheep?" enquired the little boy.

"They will make coats of it, to keep themselves warm."

"I wish I had some wool," said the boy, "for I need a new coat very badly, and mamma is so poor she cannot buy me one."

"That is too bad," replied the Black Sheep; "but I shall have more wool by and by, and then I will give you a bagful to make a new coat from."

"Will you really?" asked the boy, looking very much pleased.

"Indeed I will," answered the sheep, "for you are always kind and have a pleasant word for me. So you watch until my wool grows again, and then you shall have your share of it."

"Oh, thank you!" said the boy, and he ran away to tell his mother what the Black Sheep had said.

When the farmer came into the field again the Black Sheep said to him,

"Master, how many bags of wool did you cut from my back?"

"Two bags full," replied the farmer; "and it was very nice wool indeed."

"If I grow three bags full the next time, may I have one bag for myself?" asked the sheep.

"Why, what could you do with a bag of wool?" questioned the farmer.

The Black Sheep

"I want to give it to the little boy that lives in the lane. He is very poor and needs a new coat."

"Very well," answered the master; "if you can grow three bags full I will give one to the little boy."

So the Black Sheep began to grow wool, and tried in every way to grow the finest and heaviest fleece in all the flock. She always lay in the sunniest part of the pastures, and drank from the clearest part of the brook, and ate only the young and juicy shoots of grass and the tenderest of the sheep-sorrel. And each day the little boy came to the bars and looked at the sheep and enquired how the wool was growing.

"I am getting along finely," the Black Sheep would answer, "for not one sheep in the pasture has so much wool as I have grown already."

"Can I do anything to help you?" asked the little boy.

"Not that I think of," replied the sheep, "unless you could get me a little salt. I believe salt helps the wool to grow."

So the boy ran to the house and begged his mother for a handful of salt, and then he came back to the bars, where the Black Sheep licked it out of his hand.

Day by day the wool on the sheep grew longer and longer, and even the old ram noticed it and said,

"You are foolish to grow so much wool, for the farmer will cut it all off, and it will do you no good. Now I am growing just as little as possible, for since he steals what I have I am determined he shall get very little wool from my back."

The Black Sheep did not reply to this, for she thought the old ram very ill-tempered and selfish, and believed he was doing wrong not to grow more wool.

Finally the time came to shear the sheep again, and the farmer and his man came into the pasture to look at them, and were surprised to see what a fine, big fleece the Black Sheep had grown.

"There will be three bagsful at the least," said the master, "and I will keep my promise and give one to the little boy in the lane. But, my goodness! how scraggly and poor the old ram looks. There is scarcely any wool on him at all. I think I must sell him to the butcher!"

And, in truth, although the ram kicked and struggled and bleated with rage, they tied his legs and put him into the cart and carried him away to the butcher. And that was the last the sheep ever saw of him.

But the Black Sheep ran up to the bars by the lane and waited with a glad heart till the little boy came. When he saw the sheep waiting for him he asked,

> "Black Sheep, Black Sheep, have you any wool?"

And the sheep replied,

> "Yes my little master, three bags full!"

"That is fine!" said the boy; "but who are the three bags for?"

"One for my master, one for his dame,
And one for the little boy that lives in the lane."

"Thank you, Black Sheep," said the little boy; "you are very kind, and I shall always think of you when I wear my new coat."

The next day the sheep were all sheared, and the Black Sheep's fleece made three big bagsful. The farmer kept his promise and carried one bag to the little boy that lived in the lane, and the wool was so soft and so heavy that there was enough not only for the new coat, but to make his mother a warm dress as well.

The Black Sheep was very proud and happy when the mother and her little boy came down to the bars and showed the new clothes that had been made from the wool.

"This pays me for all my trouble," said the Black Sheep, and the little boy reached his hand through the bars and patted her gently upon the head.

Old King Cole

Old King Cole

Old King Cole was a merry old soul,
  And a merry old soul was he;
He called for his pipe and he called for his bowl
  And he called for his fiddlers three.

Old King Cole

OLD KING COLE was not always a king, nor was he born a member of any royal family. It was only chance—"hard luck" he used to call it—that made him a king at all.

He had always been a poor man, being the son of an apple peddler, who died and left him nothing but a donkey and a fiddle. But that was enough for Cole, who never bothered his head about the world's goods, but took things as they came and refused to worry about anything.

So, when the house he lived in, and the furniture, and even the apple-cart were sold to pay his father's debts, and he found himself left with the old fiddle that nobody wanted and the old donkey that no one would have—it being both vicious and unruly—he uttered no word of complaint. He simply straddled the donkey and took the fiddle under his arm and rode out into the world to seek his fortune.

When he came to a village he played a merry tune

upon the fiddle and sang a merry song with it, and the people gave him food most willingly. There was no trouble about a place to sleep, for if he was denied a bed he lay down with the donkey in a barn, or even on the village green, and making a pillow of the donkey's neck he slept as soundly as anyone could in a bed of down.

And so he continued riding along and playing upon his fiddle for many years, until his head grew bald and his face was wrinkled and his bushy eyebrows became as white as snow. But his eyes never lost their merry twinkle, and he was just as fat and hearty as in his younger days, while, if you heard him singing his songs and scraping upon the old fiddle, you would know at once his heart was as young as ever.

He never guided the donkey, but let the beast go where it would, and so it happened that at last they came to Whatland, and entered one day the city where resided the King of that great country.

Now, even as Cole rode in upon his donkey the King of Whatland lay dying in his palace, surrounded by all the luxury of the court. And as he left no heir, and was the last of the royal line, the councilors and wise men of Whatland were in a great quandary as to who should succeed him. But finally they bethought themselves of the laws of the land, and upon looking up the records they found in an old book a law that provided for just such a case as this.

"If the King dies," so read the law, "and there be

no one to succeed to the throne, the prime minister shall be blinded and led from the palace into the main street of the city. And he shall stretch out his arms and walk about, and the first person he touches shall be crowned as King of the land."

The councilors were greatly pleased when they found this law, for it enabled them to solve the problem that confronted them. So when the King had breathed his last they blindfolded the prime minister and led him forth from the palace, and he began walking about with outstretched arms seeking someone to touch.

Of course the people knew nothing of this law, nor even that the old King was dead, and seeing the prime minister groping about blindfolded they kept out of his way, fearing they might be punished if he stumbled against them. But Cole was then riding along on the donkey, and did not even know it was the prime minister who was feeling about in such a funny way. So he began to laugh, and the minister, who had by this time grown tired of the game, heard the laugh and came toward the stranger and touched him, and immediately all the wise men and the councilors fell down before him and hailed him as King of Whatland!

Thus did the wandering fiddler become King Cole, and you may be sure he laughed more merrily than ever when they explained to him his good fortune.

They carried him within the palace and dressed him in purple and fine linen, and placed a crown of gold upon his bald head and a jeweled scepter in his wrinkled hand, and all this amused old King Cole very much. When he had been led to the great throne-room and placed upon the throne of gold (where the silken cushions felt very soft and pleasant after his long ride upon the donkey's sharp back) the courtiers all knelt before him and asked what commands he wished to give, since everyone in the kingdom must now obey his slightest word.

"Oh well," said the new King, "I think the first thing I would like is my old pipe. You 'll find it in the pocket of the ragged coat I took off."

One of the officers of the court at once ran for the pipe, and when it was brought King Cole filled it with tobacco from his greasy pouch and lighted it, and you can imagine what a queer sight it was to see the fat King sitting upon the rich throne, dressed in silks and satins and a golden crown, and smoking at the same time an old black pipe!

The councilors looked at each other in dismay, and the ladies of the court sneezed and coughed and seemed greatly shocked, and all this pleased old King Cole so much that he lay back in his throne and roared with laughter.

Then the prime minister came forward very gravely, and bowing low he said,

"May it please your Majesty, it is not the custom

Old King Cole

of Kings to smoke a pipe while seated upon the throne."

"But it is my custom," answered Cole.

"It is impolite, and—unkingly!" ventured the minister.

"Now, see here, old fellow," replied his Majesty, "I did n't ask to be King of this country; it 's all your own doing. All my life I have smoked whenever I wished, and if I can't do as I please here, why, I won't be king—so there!"

"But you must be the King, your Majesty, whether you want to or not. The law says so."

"If that 's the case," returned the King, "I can do as I please in other things. So you just run and get me a bowl of punch, there 's a good fellow."

The aged minister did not like to be addressed thus, but the King's commands must be obeyed; so, although the court was greatly horrified, he brought the bowl of punch, and the King pushed his crown onto the back of his head and drank heartily, and smacked his lips afterwards.

"That 's fine!" he said; "but say—what do you people do to amuse yourselves?"

"Whatever your Majesty commands," answered one of the councilors.

"What! must I amuse you as well as myself? Methinks it is no easy task to be a King if so many things are required of me. But I suppose it is useless to fret, since the law obliges me to reign in this great country against my will. Therefore will I make the best of my misfortune, and propose we have a dance, and forget our cares. Send at once for some fiddlers, and clear the room for our merry-making, and for once in our lives we shall have a jolly good time!"

So one of the officers of the court went out and soon returned with three fiddlers, and when at the King's command they struck up a tune, the monarch was delighted, for every fiddler had a very fine fiddle and knew well how to use it.

Now, Old King Cole was a merry old soul, so he soon set all the ladies and gentlemen of the court to dancing, and he himself took off his crown and his ermine robe and laid them upon the throne, while he danced with the prettiest lady present till he was all out of breath.

Then he dismissed them, and they were all very well pleased with the new King, for they saw that, in spite of his odd ways, he had a kind heart, and would try to make every one about him as merry as he was himself.

The next morning the King was informed that several of his subjects craved audience with him, as there were matters of dispute between them that must be settled. King Cole at first refused to see them, declaring he knew nothing of the quarrels of his subjects and they must manage their own affairs; but when the prime minister told him it was one of his duties as king, and the law required it, he could not do otherwise than submit. So he put on his crown and his ermine robe and sat upon the throne, although he grumbled a good deal at the necessity; for never having had any business of his own to attend to he thought it doubly hard that in his old age he must attend to the business of others.

The first case of dispute was between two men who each claimed to own a fine cow, and after hearing the evidence, the King ordered the cow to be killed and roasted and given to the poor, since that was the easiest way to decide the matter. Then followed a quarrel between two subjects over ten pieces of gold, one claiming the other owed him that sum. The King, thinking them both rascals, ordered the gold to be paid, and then he took it and scattered it amongst the beggars outside the palace.

By this time King Cole decided he had transacted enough business for one day, so he sent word to those outside that if anyone had a quarrel that was not just he should be severely punished; and, indeed, when the subjects learned the manner in which the King settled disputes, they were afraid to come to him, as both sides were sure to be losers by the decision. And that saved King Cole a lot of trouble thereafter, for the people thought best to settle their own differences.

The King, now seeing he was free to do as he pleased, retired to his private chamber, where he called for the three fiddlers and made them play for him while he smoked his pipe and drank a bowl of punch.

Every evening he had a dance in the palace, and every day there were picnics and merry-makings of all kinds, and before long King Cole had the reputation of having the merriest court in all the world.

He loved to feast and to smoke and to drink his punch, and he was never so merry as when others were merry with him, so that the three fiddlers were almost always by his side, and at any hour of the day you could hear sweet strains of music echoing through the palace.

Old King Cole did not forget the donkey that had been his constant companion for so long. He had a golden saddle made for him, with a saddle-cloth broidered in gold and silver, and the bridle was studded with diamonds and precious stones, all taken from the King's treasury.

And when he rode out, the old fat King always bestrode the donkey, while his courtiers rode on either side of him upon their prancing chargers.

Old King Cole reigned for many years, and was generally beloved by his subjects; for he always gave liberally to all who asked, and was always as merry and happy as the day was long.

When he died the new King was found to be of a very different temper, and ruled the country with great severity; but this only served to make the memory of Old King Cole more tenderly cherished by his people, and they often sighed when they recalled his merry pranks, and the good times they enjoyed under his rule.

Mistress Mary

Mistress Mary

Mistress Mary, quite contrary,
  How does your garden grow?
With dingle bells and cockle shells
  And cowslips, all in a row.

Mistress Mary

HIGH upon a cliff that overlooked the sea was a little white cottage, in which dwelt a sailor and his wife, with their two strong sons and a little girl. The sons were also sailors, and had made several voyages with their father in a pretty ship called the "Skylark." Their names were Hobart and Robart. The little girl's name was Mary, and she was very happy indeed when her father and her brothers were at home, for they petted her and played games with, her and loved her very dearly. But when the "Skylark" went to sea, and her mother and herself were left alone in the little white cottage, the hours were very dull and tedious, and Mary counted the days until the sailors came home again.

One spring, just as the grasses began to grow green upon the cliff and the trees were dressing their stiff, barren branches in robes of delicate foliage, the father and brothers bade good-bye to Mary and her mother, for they were starting upon a voyage to the Black Sea.

"And how long will you be gone, papa?" asked

Mary, who was perched upon her father's knee, where she could nestle her soft cheek against his bushy whiskers.

"How long?" he repeated, stroking her curls tenderly as he spoke; "well, well, my darling, it will be a long time indeed! Do you know the cowslips that grow in the pastures, Mary?"

"Oh, yes; I watch for them every spring," she answered.

"And do you know the dingle-bells that grow near the edge of the wood?" he asked again.

"I know them well, papa," replied Mary, "for often I gather their blue blossoms and put them in a vase upon the table."

"And how about the cockle-shells?"

"Them also I know," said Mary eagerly, for she was glad her father should find her so well acquainted with the field flowers; "there is nothing prettier than the big white flowers of the cockle-shells. But tell me, papa, what have the flowers to do with your coming home?"

"Why, just this, sweetheart," returned the sailor gravely; "all the time that it takes the cowslips and dingle-bells and cockle-shells to sprout from the ground, and grow big and strong, and blossom into flower, and, yes—to wither and die away again—all that time shall your brothers and I sail the seas. But when the cold winds begin to blow, and the flowers are gone, then, God willing, we shall come back to you; and by that time you may have grown wiser and bigger, and I am sure you will have grown older. So one more kiss, sweetheart, and then we must go, for our time is up."

The next morning, when Mary and her mother had dried their eyes, which had been wet with grief at the departure of their loved ones, the little girl asked earnestly,

"Mamma, may I make a flower-garden?"

"A flower-garden!" repeated her mother in surprise; "why do you wish a flower-garden, Mary?"

"I want to plant in it the cockle-shells and the cowslips and the dingle-bells," she answered.

And her mother, who had heard what the sailor had said to his little girl, knew at once what Mary meant; so she kissed her daughter and replied,

"Yes, Mary, you may have the flower-garden, if you wish. We will dig a nice little bed just at the side of the house, and you shall plant your flowers and care for them yourself."

"I think I'd rather have the flowers at the front of the house," said Mary.

"But why?" enquired her mother; "they will be better sheltered at the side."

"I want them in front," persisted Mary, "for the sun shines stronger there."

"Very well," answered her mother, "make your garden at the front, if you will, and I will help you to dig up the ground."

"But I do n't want you to help," said Mary, "for this is to be my own little flower-garden, and I want to do all the work myself."

Now I must tell you that this little girl, although very sweet in many ways, had one serious fault. She was inclined to be a bit contrary, and put her own opinions and ideas before those of her elders. Perhaps Mary meant no wrong in this; she often thought she knew better how to do a thing than others did; and in such a case she was not only contrary, but anxious to have her own way.

And so her mother, who did not like her little daughter to be unhappy, often gave way to her in small things, and now she permitted Mary to make her own garden, and plant it as she would.

So Mary made a long, narrow bed at the front of the house, and then she prepared to plant her flowers.

"If you scatter the seeds," said her mother, "the flower-bed will look very pretty."

Now this was what Mary was about to do; but since her mother advised it, she tried to think of another way, for, as I said, she was contrary at times. And in the end she planted the dingle-bells all in one straight row, and the cockle-shells in another straight row the length of the bed, and she finished by planting the cowslips in another long row at the back.

Her mother smiled, but said nothing; and now, as the days passed by, Mary watered and tended her garden with great care; and when the flowers began to sprout she plucked all the weeds that grew among them, and so in the mild spring weather the plants grew finely.

"When they have grown up big and strong," said Mary one morning, as she weeded the bed, "and when they have budded and blossomed and faded away again, then papa and my brothers will come home. And I shall call the cockle-shells papa, for they are the biggest and strongest; and the dingle-bells shall be brother Hobart, and the cowslips brother Robart. And now I feel as if the flowers were really my dear ones, and I must be very careful that they come to no harm!"

She was filled with joy when one morning she ran out to her flower-garden after breakfast and found the dingle-bells and cowslips were actually blossoming, while even the cockle-shells were showing their white buds. They looked rather comical, all standing in stiff, straight rows, one after the other; but Mary did not mind that.

While she was working she heard the tramp of a horse's hoofs, and looking up saw the big bluff Squire riding toward her. The big Squire was very fond of children, and whenever he rode near the little white cottage he stopped to have a word with Mary. He was old and bald-headed, and he had side-whiskers that were very red in color and very short and stubby; but there was ever a merrry twinkle in his blue eyes, and Mary well knew him for her friend.

Now, when she looked up and saw him coming toward her flower-garden, she nodded and smiled at him, and the big bluff Squire rode up to her side, and looked down with a smile at her flowers.

Then he said to her in rhyme (for it was a way of speaking the jolly Squire had),

"Mistress Mary, so contrary,
How does your garden grow?
With dingle-bells and cockle-shells
And cowslips all in a row!"

And Mary, being a sharp little girl, and knowing the Squire's queer ways, replied to him likewise in rhyme, saying,

"I thank you, Squire, that you enquire
How well the flowers are growing;
The dingle-bells and cockle-shells
And cowslips all are blowing!"

The Squire laughed at this reply, and patted her upon her head, and then he continued,

"'T is aptly said. But prithee, maid,
Why thus your garden fill
When ev'ry field the same flowers yield
To pluck them as you will?"

"That is a long story, Squire," said Mary; "but this much I may tell you,

"The cockle-shell is father's flower,
The cowslip here is Robart,
The dingle-bell, I now must tell,
I've named for Brother Hobart.

"And when the flowers have lived their lives
  In sunshine and in rain,
And then do fade, why, papa said
  He'd sure come home again."

"Oh, that's the idea, is it?" asked the big bluff Squire, forgetting his poetry. "Well, it's a pretty thought, my child, and I think because the flowers are strong and hearty that you may know your father and brothers are the same; and I'm sure I hope they'll come back from their voyage safe and sound. I shall come and see you again, little one, and watch the garden grow." And then he said "gee-up" to his gray mare, and rode away.

The very next day, to Mary's great surprise and grief, she found the leaves of the dingle-bells curling and beginning to wither.

"Oh, mamma," she called, "come quick! Something is surely the matter with brother Hobart!"

"The dingle-bells are dying," said her mother, after looking carefully at the flowers; "but the reason is that the cold winds from the sea swept right over your garden last night, and dingle-bells are delicate flowers and grow best where they are sheltered by the woods. If you had planted them at the side of the house, as I wished you to, the wind would not have killed them."

Mary did not reply to this, but sat down and began to weep, feeling at the same time that her mother was right and it was her own fault for being so contrary.

While she sat thus the Squire rode up, and called to her

> "Fie, Mary, fie! Why do you cry,
> And blind your eyes to knowing
> How dingle-bells and cockle-shells
> And cowslips all are growing?"

"Oh, Squire!" sobbed Mary, "I am in great trouble.

> "Each dingle-bell I loved so well
> Before my eyes is dying,
> And much I fear my brother dear
> In sickness now is lying!"

"Nonsense!" said the Squire; "because you named the flowers after your brother Hobart is no reason he should be affected by the fading of the dingle-bells. I very much suspect the real reason they are dying is because the cold sea wind caught them last night. Dingle-bells are delicate. If you had scattered the cockle-shells and cowslips all about them, the stronger plants would have protected the weaker; but you see, my girl, you planted the dingle-bells all in a row, and so the wind caught them nicely."

Again Mary reproached herself for having been contrary and refusing to listen to her mother's advice; but the Squire's words comforted her, nevertheless, and made her feel that brother Hobart and the flowers had really nothing to do with each other.

The weather now began to change, and the cold sea winds blew each night over Mary's garden. She did not know this, for she was always lying snugly tucked up in her bed, and the warm morning sun usually drove away the winds; but her mother knew it, and feared Mary's garden would suffer.

One day Mary came into the house where her mother was at work and said, gleefully,

"Papa and my brothers will soon be home now."

"Why do you think so?" asked her mother.

"Because the cockle-shells and cowslips are both fading away and dying, just as the dingle-bells did, and papa said when they faded and withered he and the boys would come back to us."

Mary's mother knew that the harsh winds had killed the flowers before their time, but she did not like to disappoint her darling, so she only said, with a sigh,

"I hope you are right, Mary, for we both shall be glad to welcome our dear ones home again."

But soon afterward the big bluff Squire came riding up, as was his wont, to where Mary stood by her garden, and he at once asked,

"Pray tell me, dear, though much I fear
The answer sad I know,
How grow the sturdy cockle-shells
And cowslips, all in a row?"

And Mary looked up at him with her bright smile and answered,

"Dingle-bells and cockle-shells
And cowslips are all dead,
And now my papa 's coming home,
For so he surely said."

"Ah," said the Squire, looking at her curiously, "I 'm afraid you are getting way ahead of time. See here, Mary, how would you like a little ride with me on my nag?"

"I would like it very much, sir," replied Mary.

"Then reach up your hand. Now!—there you are, little one!" and Mary found herself seated safely in front of the Squire, who clasped her with one strong arm so that she could not slip off.

"Now, then," he said, "we'll take a little ride down the hill and by the path that runs beside the wood."

So he gave the rein to his mare and they rode along, chatting merrily together, till they came to the wood. Then said the Squire,

"Take a look within that nook
And tell me what is there."

And Mary exclaimed,

"A dingle-bell, and truth to tell
In full bloom, I declare!"

The Squire now clucked to his nag, and as they rode away he said,

"Now come with me and you shall see
A field with cowslips bright,
And not a garden in the land
Can show so fair a sight."

And so it was, for as they rode through the pastures the cowslips bloomed on every hand, and Mary's eyes grew bigger and bigger as she thought of her poor garden with its dead flowers.

And then the Squire took her toward the little brook that wandered through the meadows, flowing over the pebbles with a soft, gurgling sound that was very nearly as sweet as music; and when they reached it the big Squire said,

"If you will look beside the brook
You'll see, I know quite well,
That hidden in each mossy nook
Is many a cockle-shell."

This was indeed true, and as Mary saw them she suddenly dropped her head and began to weep.

"What's the matter, little one?" asked the Squire in his kind, bluff voice. And Mary answered,

"Although the flowers I much admire,
You know papa did say
He won't be home again, Squire,
Till all have passed away."

"You must be patient, my child," replied her friend; "and surely you would not have been thus disappointed had you not tried to make the field flowers grow where they do not belong. Gardens are all well enough for fancy flowers to grow in, but the posies that God gave to all the world, and made to grow wild in the great garden of Nature, will never thrive in other places. Your father meant you to watch the flowers in the field; and if you will come and visit them each day, you will find the time of waiting very short indeed."

Mary dried her eyes and thanked the kindly old Squire, and after that she visited the fields each day and watched the flowers grow.

And it was not so very long, as the Squire said, before the blossoms began to wither and fall away; and finally one day Mary looked out over the sea and saw a little speck upon the waters that looked like a sail. And when it came nearer and had grown larger, both she and her mother saw that it was the "Skylark" come home again, and you can imagine how pleased and happy the sight of the pretty little ship made them.

And soon after, when Mary had been hugged by her two sunburned brothers and was clasped in her father's strong arms, she whispered,

"I knew you were coming soon, papa."

"And how did you know, sweetheart?" he asked, giving her an extra kiss.

"Because I watched the flowers; and the dingle-bells and cowslips and cockle-shells are all withered and faded away. And did you not say that, God willing, when this happened you would come back to us?"

"To be sure I did," answered her father, with a happy laugh; "and I must have spoken truly, sweet-heart, for God in His goodness was willing, and here I am!"

The Wond'rous
Wise Man

The Wond'rous Wise Man

There was a man in our town
  And he was wond'rous wise;
He jumped into a bramble bush
  And scratched out both his eyes.
And when he saw his eyes were out,
  With all his might and main
He jumped into another bush
  And scratched them in again!

OUR town is a quiet little town, and lies nestling in a little valley surrounded by pretty green hills. I do not think you would ever have heard our town mentioned had not the man lived there who was so wise that everyone marvelled at his great knowledge.

He was not always a wise man; he was a wise boy before he grew to manhood, and even when a child he was so remarkable for his wisdom that people shook their heads gravely and said, "when he grows up there will be no need of books, for he will know everything!"

His father thought he had a wond'rous wise look when he was born, and so he named him Solomon, thinking that if indeed he turned out to be wise the name would fit him nicely, whereas, should he be mistaken, and the boy grow up stupid, his name could be easily changed to Simon.

But the father was not mistaken, and the boy's name remained Solomon.

When he was still a child Solomon confounded the schoolmaster by asking, one day,

"Can you tell me, sir, why a cow drinks water from a brook?"

"Well really," replied the abashed schoolmaster, "I have never given the subject serious thought. But I will sleep upon the question, and try to give you an answer to-morrow."

But the schoolmaster could not sleep; he remained awake all the night trying to think why a cow drinks water from a brook, and in the morning he was no nearer the answer than before. So he was obliged to appear before the wise child and acknowledge that he could not solve the problem.

"I have looked at the subject from every side," said he, "and given it careful thought, and yet I cannot tell why a cow drinks water from a brook."

"Sir," replied the wise child, "it is because the cow is thirsty."

The shock of this answer was so great that the schoolmaster fainted away, and when they had brought him to he made a prophecy that Solomon would grow up to be a wond'rous wise man.

It was the same way with the village doctor. Solomon came to him one day and asked,

"Tell me, sir, why has a man two eyes?"

"Bless me!" exclaimed the doctor, "I must think a bit before I answer, for I have never yet had my attention called to this subject."

So he thought for a long time, and then he said,

"I must really give it up. I cannot tell, for the life of me, why a man has two eyes. Do you know?"

"Yes, sir," answered the boy.

"Then," said the doctor, after taking a dose of quinine to brace up his nerves, for he remembered the fate of the schoolmaster, "then please tell me why a man has two eyes."

"A man has two eyes, sir," returned Solomon, solemnly, "because he was born that way."

And the doctor marvelled greatly at so much wisdom in a little child, and made a note of it in his note-book.

Solomon was so full of wisdom that it flowed from his mouth in a perfect stream, and every day he gave new evidence to his friends that he could scarcely hold all the wise thoughts that came to him. For instance, one day he said to his father,

"I perceive our dog has six legs."

"Oh, no!" replied his father, "our dog has only four legs."

"You are surely mistaken, sir," said Solomon, with the gravity that comes from great wisdom, "these are our dog's fore legs, are they not?" pointing to the front legs of the dog.

"Yes," answered his father.

"Well, continued Solomon, "the dog has two other legs, besides, and two and four are six; therefore the dog has six legs."

"But that is very old," exclaimed his father.

"True," replied Solomon, "but this is a young dog."

Then his father bowed his head in shame that his own child should teach him wisdom.

Of course Solomon wore glasses upon his eyes—all wise people wear them,—and his face was ever grave and solemn, while he walked slowly and stiffly so that people might know he was the celebrated wise man, and do him reverence.

And when he had grown to manhood the fame of his wisdom spread all over the world, so that all the other wise men were jealous, and tried in many ways to confound him; but Solomon always came out ahead and maintained his reputation for wisdom.

Finally a very wise man came from Cumberland, to meet Solomon and see which of them was the wisest. He was a very big man, and Solomon was a very little man, and so the people all shook their heads sadly and feared Solomon had met his match, for if the Cumberland man was as full of wisdom as Solomon, he had much the advantage in size.

They formed a circle around the two wise men, and then began the trial to see which was the wisest.

"Tell me," said Solomon, looking straight up into

The Wond'rous Wise Man

the big man's face with an air of confidence that reassured his friends, "how many sisters has a boy who has one father, one mother, and seven brothers?"

The big wise man got very red in the face, and scowled and coughed and stammered, but he could not tell.

"I do not know," he acknowledged; "nor do you know, either, for there is no rule to go by."

"Oh, yes, I know," replied Solomon; "he has two sisters. I know this is the true answer, because I know the boy and his father and his mother and his brothers and his sisters, so that I cannot be mistaken."

Now all the people applauded at this, for they were sure Solomon had got the best of the man from Cumberland.

But it was now the big man's turn to try Solomon, so he said,

"Fingers five are on my hand;
All of them upright do stand.
One a dog is, chasing kittens;
One a cat is, wearing mittens;
One a rat is, eating cheese;
One a wolf is, full of fleas;
One a fly is, in a cup—
How many fingers do I hold up?"

"Four," replied Solomon, promptly, "for one of them is a thumb!"

The wise man from Cumberland was so angry at being outwitted that he sprang at Solomon and would no doubt have injured him had not our wise man turned and run away as fast as he could go. The man from Cumberland at once ran after him, and chased him through the streets and down the lanes and up the side of the hill where the bramble-bushes grow.

Solomon ran very fast, but the man from Cumberland was bigger, and he was just about to grab our wise man by his coat-tails when Solomon gave a great jump, and jumped right into the middle of a big bramble-bush!

The people were all coming up behind, and as the big man did not dare to follow Solomon into the bramble-bush, he turned away and ran home to Cumberland.

All the men and women of our town were horrified when they came up and found their wise man in the middle of the bramble-bush, and held fast by the brambles, which scratched and pricked him on every side.

"Solomon! are you hurt?" they cried.

"I should say I am hurt!" replied Solomon, with a groan; "my eyes are scratched out!"

"How do you know they are?" asked the village doctor.

"I can see they are scratched out!" replied Solomon; and the people all wept with grief at this, and Solomon howled louder than any of them.

Now the fact was that when Solomon jumped into the bramble-bush he was wearing his spectacles, and the brambles pushed the glasses so close against his eyes that he could not open them; and so, as every other part of him was scratched and bleeding, and he could not open his eyes, he made sure they were scratched out.

"How am I to get out of here?" he asked at last.

"You must jump out," replied the doctor, "since you have jumped in."

So Solomon made a great jump, and although the brambles tore him cruelly, he sprang entirely out of the bush and fell plump into another one.

This last bush, however, by good luck, was not a bramble-bush, but one of elderberry, and when he jumped into it his spectacles fell off, and to his surprise he opened his eyes and found that he could see again.

"Where are you now?" called out the doctor.

"I'm in the elderberry bush, and I've scratched my eyes in again!" answered Solomon.

When the people heard this they marvelled greatly at the wisdom of a man who knew how to scratch his eyes in after they were scratched out; and they lifted Solomon from the bush and carried him home, where they bound up the scratches and nursed him carefully until he was well again.

And after that no one ever questioned the wond'rous wisdom of our wise man, and when he finally died, at a good old age, they built a great monument over his grave, and on one side of it were the words,

"Solomon; the Man who was Wond'rous Wise."

and on the other side was a picture of a bramble-bush.

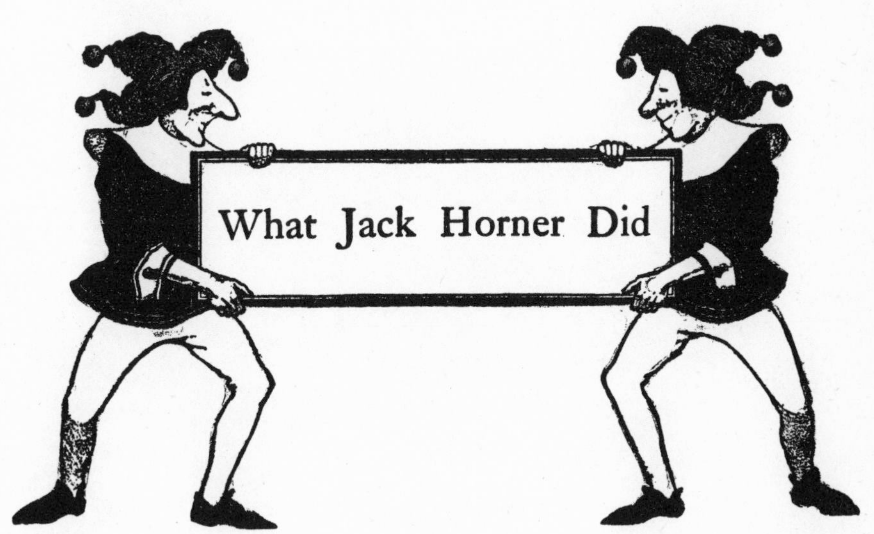
What Jack Horner Did

What Jack Horner Did

Little Jack Horner sat in a corner,
  Eating a Christmas pie;
He put in his thumb and pulled out a plum
  And said, "What a good boy am I!"

What Jack Horner Did

LITTLE JACK HORNER lived in an old, tumble-down house at the edge of a big wood; and there many generations of Horners had lived before him, and had earned their living by chopping wood. Jack's father and mother were both dead, and he lived with his grandfather and grandmother, who took great pains to teach him all that a boy should know.

They lived very comfortably and happily together until one day a great tree fell upon Grandpa Horner and crushed his legs; and from that time on he could not work at all, but had to be nursed and tended very carefully.

This calamity was a great affliction to the Horners. Grandma Horner had a little money saved up in an old broken teapot that she kept in the cupboard, but that would not last them a great time, and when it was gone they would have nothing with which to buy food.

"I 'm sure I do n't know what is to become of us," she said to Jack, "for I am too old to work, and you are too young." She always told her troubles to Jack now; small though he was, he was the only one she could talk freely with, since it would only bother the poor crippled grandfather to tell him how low the money was getting in the teapot.

"It is true," replied Jack, "that you are too old to work, for your rheumatism will barely allow you to care for the house and cook our meals; and there is grandpa to be tended. But I am not too young to work, grandma, and I shall take my little hatchet and go into the wood. I cannot cut the big trees, but I can the smaller ones, and I am sure I shall be able to pile up enough wood to secure the money we need for food."

"You are a good boy, dear," said grandma Horner, patting his head lovingly, "but you are too young for the task. We must think of some other way to keep the wolf from the door."

But Jack was not shaken in his resolve, although he saw it was useless to argue further with his grandmother. So the next morning he rose very early and took his little axe and went into the wood to begin his work. There were a good many branches scattered about, and these he was able to cut with ease; and then he piled them up nicely to be sold when the wood-carter next came around. When dinner-time came he stopped long enough to eat some of the bread and cheese he had brought with him, and then he resumed his work.

But scarcely had he chopped one branch when a faint cry from the wood arrested his attention. It seemed as if some one was shouting for help. Jack listened a moment, and again heard the cry.

Without hesitation he seized his axe and ran toward the place from whence the cry had proceeded. The underbrush was very thick and the thorns caught in his clothing and held him back, but with the aid of his sharp little axe he overcame all difficulties and presently reached a place where the wood was more open.

He paused here, for often he had been told by Grandpa Horner that there were treacherous bogs in this part of the wood, which were so covered with mosses and ferns that the ground seemed solid enough to walk upon. But woe to the unlucky traveler who stepped unawares upon their surface; for instantly he found himself caught by the clinging moist clay, to sink farther and farther into the bog until, swallowed up in the mire, he would meet a horrible death beneath its slimy surface. His grandfather had told him never to go near these terrible bogs, and Jack, who was an obedient boy, had always kept away from this part of the wood. But as he paused, again that despairing cry came to his ears, very near to him now, it seemed:

"Help!"

Forgetful of all save a desire to assist this unknown

sufferer, Jack sprang forward with an answering cry, and only halted when he found himself upon the edge of a vast bog.

"Where are you?" he then shouted.

"Here!" answered a voice, and, looking down, Jack saw, a few feet away, the head and shoulders of a man. He had walked into the bog and sunk into its treacherous depths nearly to his waist, and, although he struggled bravely, his efforts only seemed to draw him farther down toward a frightful death.

For a moment, filled with horror and dismay, Jack stood looking at the man. Then he remembered a story he had once heard of how a man had been saved from the bog.

"Be quiet, sir!" he called to the unfortunate stranger; "save all your strength, and I may yet be able to rescue you."

He then ran to a tall sapling that stood near and began chopping away with his axe. The keen blade speedily cut through the young but tough wood, and, then Jack dragged it to the edge of the bog, and, exerting all his strength, pushed it out until the sapling was within reach of the sinking man.

"Grab it, sir!" he called out, "and hold on tightly. It will keep you from sinking farther into the mire, and when you have gained more strength you may be able to pull yourself out."

"You are a brave boy," replied the stranger, "and I shall do as you tell me."

Jack Horner

It was a long and tedious struggle, and often Jack thought the stranger would despair and be unable to drag his body from the firm clutch of the bog; but little by little the man succeeded in drawing himself up by the sapling, and at last he was saved, and sank down exhausted upon the firm ground by Jack's side.

The boy then ran for some water that stood in a slough near by, and with this he bathed the stranger's face and cooled his parched lips. Then he gave him the remains of his bread and cheese, and soon the gentleman became strong enough to walk with Jack's help to the cottage at the edge of the wood.

Grandma Horner was greatly surprised to see the strange man approaching, supported by her sturdy little grandson; but she ran to help him, and afterward gave him some old clothing of Grandpa Horner's to replace his own muddy garments. When the man had fully rested, she brewed him her last bit of tea, and by that time the stranger declared he felt as good as new.

"Is this your son, ma'am?" he asked, pointing to Jack.

"He is my grandson, sir," answered the woman.

"He is a good boy," declared the stranger, "and a brave boy as well, for he has saved my life. I live far away in a big city, and have plenty of money. If you will give Jack to me I will take him home and educate him, and make a great man of him when he grows up."

Grandma Horner hesitated, for the boy was very dear to her and the pride of her old age; but Jack spoke up for himself.

"I'll not go," he said, stoutly; "you are very kind, and mean well by me, but grandma and grandpa have only me to care for them now, and I must stay with them and cut the wood, and so keep them supplied with food."

The stranger said nothing more, but he patted Jack's head kindly, and soon after left them and took the road to the city.

The next morning Jack went to the wood again, and began chopping as bravely as before. And by hard work he cut a great deal of wood, which the wood-carter carried away and sold for him. The pay was not very much, to be sure, but Jack was glad that he was able to earn something to help his grandparents.

And so the days passed rapidly away until it was nearly Christmas time, and now, in spite of Jack's earnings, the money was very low indeed in the broken teapot.

One day, just before Christmas, a great wagon drove up to the door of the little cottage, and in it was the stranger Jack had rescued from the bog. The wagon was loaded with a store of good things which would add to the comfort of the aged pair and their grandson, including medicines for grandpa and rare teas for grandma, and a fine suit of clothes for Jack, who was just then away at work in the wood.

When the stranger had brought all these things into the house, he asked to see the old teapot. Trembling with the excitement of their good fortune, Grandma Horner brought out the teapot, and the gentleman drew a bag from beneath his coat and filled the pot to the brim with shining gold pieces.

"If ever you need more," he said, "send to me, and you shall have all you wish to make you comfortable."

Then he told her his name, and where he lived, so that she might find him if need be, and then he drove away in the empty wagon before Grandma Horner had half finished thanking him.

You can imagine how astonished and happy little Jack was when he returned from his work and found all the good things his kind benefactor had brought. Grandma Horner was herself so delighted that she caught the boy in her arms, and hugged and kissed him, declaring that his brave rescue of the gentleman had brought them all this happiness in their hour of need.

"To-morrow is Christmas," she said, "and we shall have an abundance with which to celebrate the good day. So I shall make you a Christmas pie, Jack dear, and stuff it full of plums, for you must have your share of our unexpected prosperity."

And Grandma Horner was as good as her word, and made a very delicious pie indeed for her darling grandson.

And this was how it came that

"Little Jack Horner sat in a corner
Eating a Christmas pie;
He put in his thumb and pulled out a plum,
And said, "What a good boy am I!"

And he was—a very good boy. Do n't you think so?

The Man in the Moon

The Man in the Moon

The Man in the Moon came tumbling down,
  And enquired the way to Norwich;
He went by the south and burned his mouth
  With eating cold pease porridge!

WHAT! have you never heard the story of the Man in the Moon? Then I must surely tell it, for it is very amusing, and there is not a word of truth in it.

The Man in the Moon was rather lonesome, and often he peeked over the edge of the moon and looked down upon the earth and envied all the people who lived together, for he thought it must be vastly more pleasant to have companions to talk to than to be shut up in a big planet all by himself, where he had to whistle to keep himself company.

One day he looked down and saw an alderman sailing up through the air towards him. This alderman was being translated (instead of being transported, owing to a misprint in the law) and as he came near the Man in the Moon called to him and said,

"How is everything down on the earth?"

"Everything is lovely," replied the alderman, "and I would n't leave it if I was not obliged to."

"What's a good place to visit down there?" enquired the Man in the Moon.

"Oh, Norwich is a mighty fine place," returned the alderman, "and it's famous for its pease porridge;" and then he sailed out of sight and left the Man in the Moon to reflect upon what he had said.

The words of the alderman made him more anxious than ever to visit the earth, and so he walked thoughtfully home, and put a few lumps of ice in the stove to keep him warm, and sat down to think how he should manage the trip.

You see, everything went by contraries in the Moon, and when the Man wished to keep warm he knocked off a few chunks of ice and put them in his stove; and he cooled his drinking water by throwing red-hot coals of fire into the pitcher. Likewise, when he became chilly he took off his hat and coat, and even his shoes, and so became warm; and in the hot days of summer he put on his overcoat to cool off.

All of which seems very queer to you, no doubt; but it wasn't at all queer to the Man in the Moon, for he was accustomed to it.

Well, he sat by his ice-cool fire and thought about his journey to the earth, and finally he decided the only way he could get there was to slide down a moonbeam.

So he left the house and locked the door and put the key in his pocket, for he was uncertain how long he should be gone; and then he went to the edge of the moon and began to search for a good strong moonbeam.

At last he found one that seemed rather substantial and reached right down to a pleasant-looking spot on the earth; and so he swung himself over the edge of the moon, and put both arms tight around the moonbeam and started to slide down. But he found it rather slippery, and in spite of all his efforts to hold on he found himself going faster and faster, so that just before he reached the earth he lost his hold and came tumbling down head over heels and fell plump into a river.

The cool water nearly scalded him before he could swim out, but fortunately he was near the bank and he quickly scrambled upon the land and sat down to catch his breath.

By that time it was morning, and as the sun rose its hot rays cooled him off somewhat, so that he began looking about curiously at all the strange sights and wondering where on earth he was.

By and by a farmer came along the road by the river with a team of horses drawing a load of hay, and the horses looked so odd to the Man in the Moon that at first he was greatly frightened, never before having seen horses except from his home in the moon, from whence they looked a good deal smaller. But he plucked up courage and said to the farmer,

"Can you tell me the way to Norwich, sir?"

"Norwich?" repeated the farmer musingly; "I

don't know exactly where it be, sir, but it's somewhere away to the south."

"Thank you," said the Man in the Moon.—But stop! I must not call him the Man in the Moon any longer, for of course he was now *out* of the moon; so I'll simply call him the Man, and you'll know by that which man I mean.

Well, the Man in the—I mean the Man (but I nearly forgot what I have just said)—the Man turned to the south and began walking briskly along the road, for he had made up his mind to do as the alderman had advised and travel to Norwich, that he might eat some of the famous pease porridge that was made there. And finally, after a long and tiresome journey, he reached the town and stopped at one of the first houses he came to, for by this time he was very hungry indeed.

A good-looking woman answered his knock at the door, and he asked politely,

"Is this the town of Norwich, madam?"

"Surely this is the town of Norwich," returned the woman.

"I came here to see if I could get some pease porridge," continued the Man, "for I hear you make the nicest porridge in the world in this town."

"That we do, sir," answered the woman, "and if you'll step inside I'll give you a bowl, for I have plenty in the house that is newly made."

The Man in the Moon

So he thanked her and entered the house, and she asked,

"Will you have it hot or cold, sir?"

"Oh, cold, by all means," replied the Man, "for I detest anything hot to eat."

She soon brought him a bowl of cold pease porridge, and the Man was so hungry that he took a big spoonful at once.

But no sooner had he put it into his mouth than he uttered a great yell, and began dancing frantically about the room, for of course the porridge that was cold to earth folk was hot to him, and the big spoonful of cold pease porridge had burned his mouth to a blister!

"What 's the matter?" asked the woman.

"Matter!" screamed the Man; "why, your porridge is so hot it has burned me."

"Fiddlesticks!" she replied, "the porridge is quite cold."

"Try it yourself!" he cried. So she tried it and found it very cold and pleasant. But the Man was so astonished to see her eat the porridge that had blistered his own mouth that he became frightened and ran out of the house and down the street as fast as he could go.

The policeman on the first corner saw him running, and promptly arrested him, and he was marched off to the magistrate for trial.

"What is your name?" asked the magistrate.

"I have n't any," replied the Man; for of course as he was the only Man in the Moon it was n't necessary he should have a name.

"Come, come, no nonsense!" said the magistrate, "you must have some name. Who are you?"

"Why, I'm the Man in the Moon."

"That's rubbish!" said the magistrate, eyeing the prisoner severely, "you may be a man, but you're not in the moon—you're in Norwich."

"That is true," answered the Man, who was quite bewildered by this idea.

"And of course you must be called something," continued the magistrate.

"Well, then," said the prisoner, "if I'm not the Man in the Moon I must be the Man out of the Moon; so call me that."

"Very good," replied the judge; "now, then, where did you come from?"

"The moon."

"Oh, you did, eh? How did you get here?"

"I slid down a moonbeam."

"Indeed! Well, what were you running for?"

"A woman gave me some cold pease porridge, and it burned my mouth."

The magistrate looked at him a moment in surprise, and then he said,

"This person is evidently crazy; so take him to the lunatic asylum and keep him there."

This would surely have been the fate of the Man

had there not been present an old astronomer who had often looked at the moon through his telescope, and so had discovered that what was hot on earth was cold in the moon, and what was cold here was hot there; so he began to think the Man had told the truth. Therefore he begged the magistrate to wait a few minutes while he looked through his telescope to see if the Man in the Moon was there. So, as it was now night, he fetched his telescope and looked at the Moon,—and found there was no man in it at all!

"It seems to be true," said the astronomer, "that the Man has got out of the Moon somehow or other. Let me look at your mouth, sir, and see if it is really burned."

Then the Man opened his mouth, and everyone saw plainly it was burned to a blister! Thereupon the magistrate begged his pardon for doubting his word, and asked him what he would like to do next.

"I'd like to get back to the Moon," said the Man, "for I don't like this earth of yours at all. The nights are too hot."

"Why, it's quite cool this evening!" said the magistrate.

"I'll tell you what we can do," remarked the astronomer; "there's a big balloon in town which belongs to the circus that came here last summer, and was pawned for a board bill. We can inflate this balloon and send the Man out of the Moon home in it."

"That's a good idea," replied the judge. So the

balloon was brought and inflated, and the Man got into the basket and gave the word to let go, and then the balloon mounted up into the sky in the direction of the moon.

The good people of Norwich stood on the earth and tipped back their heads, and watched the balloon go higher and higher, until finally the Man reached out and caught hold of the edge of the moon, and behold! the next minute he was the Man in the Moon again!

After this adventure he was well contented to stay at home; and I've no doubt if you look through a telescope you will see him there to this day.

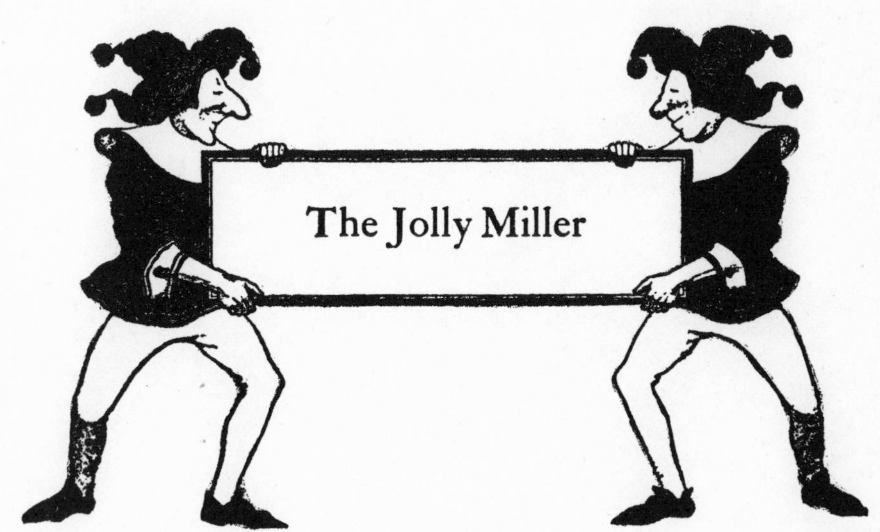
The Jolly Miller

The Jolly Miller

There was a jolly miller
  Lived on the river Dee;
He sang and worked from morn till night,
  No lark so blithe as he.
And this the burden of his song
  Forever seemed to be:
I care for nobody, no! not I,
  Since nobody cares for me.

"CREE-E-EEKETY-CRUCK-CRICK! cree-e-eekety-cruck-crick!" sang out the big wheel of the mill upon the river Dee, for it was old and ricketty and had worked many years grinding corn for the miller; so from morning till night it creaked and growled and complained as if rebelling against the work it must do. And the country people, at work in the fields far away, would raise their heads when the soft summer breezes wafted the sound of the wheel to their ears and say,

"The jolly miller is grinding his corn." And again, at the times when the mill was shut down and no sound of the wheel reached them, they said to one another,

"The jolly miller has no corn to grind to-day," or, "The miller is oiling the great wheel." But they would miss the creaking, monotonous noise, and feel more content when the mill started again and made music for them as they worked.

But no one came to the mill unless they brought corn to grind, for the miller was a queer man, and liked to be alone. When people passed by the mill and saw the miller at his work, they only nodded their heads, for they knew he would not reply if they spoke to him.

He was not an old man, nor a sour man, nor a bad man; on the contrary he could be heard singing at his work most of the time. But the words of his song would alone have kept people away from him, for they were always these:

"I care for nobody, no! not I,
Since nobody cares for me."

He iived all alone in the mill-house, cooking his own meals and making his own bed, and neither asking nor receiving help from anyone. It is very certain that if the jolly miller had cared to have friends many would have visited him, since the country people were sociable enough in their way; but it was the miller himself who refused to make friends, and old Farmer Dobson used to say,

"The reason nobody cares for the miller is because he won't let them. It is the fault of the man himself, not the fault of the people!"

However this may have been, it is true the miller

had no friends, and equally sure that he cared to have none, for it did not make him a bit unhappy.

Sometimes, indeed, as he sat at evening in the doorway of the mill and watched the moon rise in the sky, he grew a bit lonely and thoughtful, and found himself longing for some one to love and cherish, for this is the nature of all good men. But when he realized how his thoughts were straying he began to sing again, and he drove away all such hopeless longings.

At last a change came over the miller's life. He was standing one evening beside the river, watching the moonbeams play upon the water, when something came floating down the stream that attracted his attention. For a long time he could not tell what it was, but it looked to him like a big black box; so he got a long pole and reached it out towards the box and managed to draw it within reach just above the big wheel. It was fortunate he saved it when he did, for in another moment it would have gone over the wheel and been dashed to pieces far below.

When the miller had pulled the floating object upon the bank he found it really was a box, the lid being fastened tight with a strong cord. So he lifted it carefully and carried it into the mill-house, and then he placed it upon the floor while he lighted a candle. Then he cut the cord and opened the box, and behold! a little babe lay within it, sweetly sleeping upon a pillow of down.

The miller was so surprised that he stopped singing and gazed with big eyes at the beautiful face of the little stranger. And while he gazed its eyes opened—two beautiful, pleading blue eyes,—and the little one smiled and stretched out her arms toward him.

"Well, well!" said the miller, "where on earth did you come from?"

The baby did not reply, but she tried to, and made some soft little noises that sounded like the cooing of a pigeon.

The tiny arms were still stretched upwards, and the miller bent down and tenderly lifted the child from the box and placed her upon his knee, and then he began to stroke the soft, silken ringlets that clustered around her head, and to look upon her wonderingly. The baby leaned against his breast and fell asleep again, and the miller became greatly troubled, for he was unused to babies and did not know how to handle them or care for them. But he sat very still until the little one awoke, and then, thinking it must be hungry, he brought some sweet milk and fed her with a spoon.

The baby smiled at him and ate the milk as if it liked it, and then one little dimpled hand caught hold of the miller's whiskers and pulled sturdily, while the baby jumped its little body up and down and cooed its delight.

Do you think the miller was angry? Not a bit of

it! He smiled back into the laughing face and let her pull his whiskers as much as she liked. For his whole heart had gone out to this little waif that he had rescued from the river, and at last the solitary man had found something to love.

The baby slept that night in the miller's own bed, snugly tucked in beside the miller himself; and in the morning he fed her milk again, and then went out to his work singing more merrily than ever.

Every few minutes he would put his head into the room where he had left the child, to see if it wanted anything, and if it cried even the least bit he would run in and take it in his arms and soothe the little girl until she smiled again.

That first day the miller was fearful some one would come and claim the child, but when evening came without the arrival of any stranger he decided the baby had been cast adrift and now belonged to nobody but him.

"I shall keep her as long as I live," he thought, "and never will we be separated for even a day. For now that I have found some one to love I could not bear to let her go again."

He cared for the waif very tenderly; and as the child was strong and healthy she was not much trouble to him, and to his delight grew bigger day by day.

The country people were filled with surprise when they saw a child in the mill-house, and wondered where it came from; but the miller would answer no questions, and as year after year passed away they forgot to enquire how the child came there and looked upon her as the miller's own daughter.

She grew to be a sweet and pretty child, and was the miller's constant companion. She called him "papa," and he called her Nathalie, because he had found her upon the water, and the country people called her the Maid of the Mill.

The miller worked harder than ever before, for now he had to feed and clothe the little girl; and he sang from morn till night, so joyous was he, and still his song was:

> "I care for nobody, no! not I,
> Since nobody cares for me."

One day, while he was singing this, he heard a sob beside him, and looked down to see Nathalie weeping.

"What is it, my pet?" he asked, anxiously.

"Oh, papa," she answered, "why do you sing that nobody cares for you, when you know I love you so dearly?"

The miller was surprised, for he had sung the song so long he had forgotten what the words meant.

"Do you indeed love me, Nathalie?" he asked.

"Indeed, indeed! You know I do!" she replied.

"Then," said the miller, with a happy laugh, as he bent down and kissed the tear-stained face, "I shall change my song."

And after that he sang:

> "I love sweet Nathalie, that I do,
> For Nathalie she loves me."

The years passed by and the miller was very happy. Nathalie grew to be a sweet and lovely maiden, and she learned to cook the meals and tend the house, and that made it easier for the miller, for now he was growing old.

One day the young Squire, who lived at the great house on the hill, came past the mill and saw Nathalie sitting in the doorway, her pretty form framed in the flowers that climbed around and over the door.

And the Squire loved her after that first glance, for he saw that she was as good and innocent as she was beautiful. The miller, hearing the sound of voices, came out and saw them together, and at once he became very angry, for he knew that trouble was in store for him, and he must guard his treasure very carefully if he wished to keep her with him. The young Squire begged very hard to be allowed to pay court to the Maid of the Mill, but the miller ordered him away, and he was forced to go. Then the miller saw there were tears in Nathalie's eyes, and that made him still more anxious, for he feared the mischief was already done.

Indeed, in spite of the miller's watchfulness, the Squire and Nathalie often met and walked together in the shady lanes or upon the green banks of the river.

It was not long before they learned to love one another very dearly, and one day they went hand in hand to the miller and asked his consent that they should wed.

"What will become of me?" asked the miller, with a sad heart.

"You shall live in the great house with us," replied the Squire, "and never again need you labor for bread."

But the old man shook his head.

"A miller I have lived," quoth he, "and a miller will I die. But tell me, Nathalie, are you willing to leave me?"

The girl cast down her eyes and blushed sweetly.

"I love him," she whispered, "and if you separate us I shall die."

"Then," said the miller, kissing her with a heavy heart, "go; and may God bless you!"

So Nathalie and the Squire were wed, and lived in the great house, and the very day after the wedding she came walking down to the mill in her pretty new gown to see the miller.

But as she drew near she heard him singing, as was his wont; and the song he sung she had not heard since she was a little girl, for this was it:

"I care for nobody, no! not I,
Since nobody cares for me."

She came up softly behind him, and put her arms around his neck.

"Papa," said she, "you must not sing that song. Nathalie loves you yet, and always will while she lives; for my new love is complete in itself, and has not robbed you of one bit of the love that has always been your very own."

The miller turned and looked into her blue eyes, and knew that she spoke truly.

"Then I must learn a new song again," he said, "for it is lonely at the mill, and singing makes the heart lighter. But I will promise that never again, till you forget me, will I sing that nobody cares for me."

And the miller did learn a new song, and sang it right merrily for many years; for each day Nathalie came down to the mill to show that she had not forgotten him.

The Little Man and
His Little Gun

The Little Man and His Little Gun

There was a little man and he had a little gun,
  And the bullets were made of lead, lead, lead.
He went to the brook and shot a little duck,
  And the bullet went right through its head, head, head.

The Little Man and His Little Gun

THERE was once a little man named Jimson, who had stopped growing when he was a boy, and never started again. So, although he was old enough to be a man he was hardly big enough, and had he not owned a bald head and gray whiskers you would certainly have taken him for a boy whenever you saw him.

This little man was very sorry he was not bigger, and if you wanted to make him angry you had but to call attention to his size. He dressed just as big men do, and wore a silk hat and a long-tailed coat when he went to church, and a cap and top-boots when he rode horseback. He walked with a little cane and had a little umbrella made to carry when it rained. In fact, whatever other men did this little man was anxious to do also, and so it happened that when the hunting season came around, and all the men began to get their guns ready to hunt for snipe and duck, Mr. Jimson also had a little gun made, and determined to use it as well as any of them.

When he brought it home and showed it to his wife, who was a very big woman, she said,

"Jimson, you'd better use bullets made of bread, and then you won't hurt anything."

"Nonsense, Joan," replied the little man, "I shall have bullets made of lead, just as other men do, and every duck I see I shall shoot and bring home to you."

"I'm afraid you won't kill many," said Joan.

But the little man believed he could shoot with the best of them, so the next morning he got up early and took his little gun and started down to the brook to hunt for duck.

It was scarcely daybreak when he arrived at the brook, and the sun had not yet peeped over the eastern hill-tops, but no duck appeared anywhere in sight, although Mr. Jimson knew this was the right time of day for shooting them. So he sat down beside the brook and begun watching, and before he knew it he had fallen fast asleep.

By and by he was awakened by a peculiar noise.

"Quack, quack, quack!" sounded in his ears; and looking up he saw a pretty little duck swimming in the brook and popping its head under the water in search of something to eat. The duck belonged to Johnny Sprigg, who lived a little way down the brook, but the little man did not know this. He thought it was a wild duck, so he stood up and carefully took aim.

"I'm afraid I can't hit it from here," he thought,

"so I'll just step upon that big stone in the brook, and shoot from there."

So he stepped out upon the stone, and took aim at the duck again, and fired the gun.

The next minute the little man had tumbled head over heels into the water, and he nearly drowned before he could scramble out again; for, not being used to shooting, the gun had kicked, or recoiled, and had knocked him off the round stone where he had been standing.

When he had succeeded in reaching the bank he was overjoyed to see that he had shot the duck, which lay dead upon the water a short distance away. The little man got a long stick, and, reaching it out, drew the dead duck to the bank. Then he started joyfully homeward to show the prize to his wife.

"There, Joan," he said, as he entered the house, "is a nice little duck for our dinner. Do you now think your husband cannot shoot?"

"But there 's only one duck," remarked his wife, "and it 's very small. Can't you go and shoot another? Then we shall have enough for dinner."

"Yes, of course I can shoot another," said the little man, proudly; "you make a fire and get the pot boiling, and I 'll go for another duck."

"You 'd better shoot a drake this time," said Joan, "for drakes are bigger."

She started to make the fire, and the little man took his gun and went to the brook; but not a duck did he see, nor drake neither, and so he was forced to come home without any game.

"There 's no use cooking one duck," said his wife, "so we 'll have pork and beans for dinner and I 'll hang the little duck in the shed. Perhaps you 'll be able to shoot a drake to-morrow, and then we 'll cook them both together."

So they had pork and beans, to the great disappointment of Mr. Jimson, who had expected to eat duck instead; and after dinner the little man lay down to take a nap while his wife went out to tell the neighbors what a great hunter he was.

The news spread rapidly through the town, and when the evening paper came out the little man was very angry to see this verse printed in it:

There was a little man and he had a little gun,
And the bullets were made of lead, lead, lead.
He went to the brook and shot a little duck,
And the bullet went right through its head, head, head.

He carried it home to his good wife Joan,
And bade her a fire to make, make, make,
While he went to the brook where he shot the little duck,
And tried for to shoot the drake, drake, drake.

"There 's no use putting it into the paper," exclaimed the little man, much provoked, "and Mr. Brayer, the editor, is probably jealous because he himself cannot shoot a gun. Perhaps people think I cannot shoot a drake, but I 'll show them to-morrow that I can!"

So the next morning he got up early again, and

took his gun, and loaded it with bullets made of lead. Then he said to his wife,

"What does a drake look like, my love?"

"Why," she replied, "it 's much like a duck, only it has a curl on its tail and red on its wing."

"All right," he answered, "I 'll bring you home a drake in a short time, and to-day we shall have something better for dinner than pork and beans."

When he got to the brook there was nothing in sight, so he sat down on the bank to watch, and again fell fast asleep.

Now Johnny Sprigg had missed his little duck, and knew some one had shot it; so he thought this morning he would go the brook and watch for the man who had killed the duck, and make him pay a good price for it. Johnny was a big man, whose head was very bald; therefore he wore a red curly wig to cover his baldness and make him look younger.

When he got to the brook he saw no one about, and so he hid in a clump of bushes. After a time the little man woke up, and in looking around for the drake he saw Johnny's red wig sticking out of the top of the bushes.

"That is surely the drake," he thought, "for I can see a curl and something red;" and the next minute "bang!" went the gun, and Johnny Sprigg gave a great yell and jumped out of the bushes. As for his beautiful wig, it was shot right off his head, and fell into the water of the brook a good ten yards away!

"What are you trying to do?" he cried, shaking his fist at the little man.

"Why, I was only shooting at the drake," replied Jimson; "and I hit it, too, for there it is in the water."

"That 's my wig, sir!" said Johnny Sprigg, "and you shall pay for it, or I 'll have the law on you. Are you the man who shot the duck here yesterday morning?"

"I am, sir," answered the little man, proud that he had shot something besides a wig.

"Well, you shall pay for that also," said Mr. Sprigg; "for it belonged to me, and I 'll have the money or I 'll put you in jail!"

The little man did not want to go to jail, so with a heavy heart he paid for the wig and the duck, and then took his way sorrowfully homeward.

He did not tell Joan of his meeting with Mr. Sprigg; he only said he could not find a drake. But she knew all about it when the paper came out, for this is what it said on the front page:

> There was a little man and he had a little gun,
> And the bullets were made of lead, lead, lead.
> He shot Johnny Sprigg through the middle of his wig,
> And knocked it right off from his head, head, head.

The little man was so angry at this, and at the laughter of all the men he met, that he traded his gun off for a lawn-mower, and resolved never to go hunting again.

He had the little duck he had shot made into a pie, and he and Joan ate it; but he did not enjoy it very much.

"This duck cost me twelve dollars," he said to his loving wife, "for that is the sum Johnny Sprigg made me pay; and it 's a very high price for one little duck —do n't you think so, Joan?"

Hickory, Dickory, Dock

Hickory, Dickory, Dock

Hickory, Dickory, Dock!
The mouse ran up the clock.
  The clock struck one,
  The mouse ran down,
Hickory, Dickory, Dock!

Hickory, Dickory, Dock

WITHIN the hollow wall of an old brick mansion, away up the near the roof, there lived a family of mice. It was a snug little home, pleasant and quiet, and as dark as any mouse could desire. Mamma Mouse liked it because, as she said, the draught that came through the rafters made it cool in summer, and they were near enough to the chimney to keep warm in winter-time.

Besides the Mamma Mouse there were three children, named Hickory and Dickory and Dock. There had once been a Papa Mouse as well; but while he was hunting for food one night he saw a nice piece of cheese in a wire box, and attempted to get it. The minute he stuck his head into the box, however, it closed with a snap that nearly cut his head off, and when Mamma Mouse came down to look for him he was quite dead.

Mamma Mouse had to bear her bitter sorrow all alone, for the children were too young at that time to appreciate their loss. She felt that people were very cruel to kill a poor mouse for wishing to get food for himself and his family. There is nothing else for a mouse to do but take what he can find, for mice cannot earn money, as people do, and they must live in some way.

But Mamma Mouse was a brave mouse, and knew that it was now her duty to find food for her little ones; so she dried her eyes and went bravely to work gnawing through the base-board that separated the pantry from the wall. It took her some time to do this, for she could only work at night. Mice like to sleep during the day and work at night, when there are no people around to interrupt them, and even the cat is fast asleep. Some mice run about in the day-time, but they are not very wise mice who do this.

At last Mamma Mouse gnawed a hole through the base-board large enough for her to get through into the pantry, and then her disappointment was great to find the bread jar covered over with a tin pan.

"How thoughtless people are to put things where a hungry mouse cannot get at them," said Mamma Mouse to herself, with a sigh. But just then she espied a barrel of flour standing upon the floor; and that gave her new courage, for she knew she could easily gnaw through that, and the flour would do to eat just as well as the bread.

It was now nearly daylight, so she decided to leave the attack upon the flour barrel until the next night;

and gathering up for the children a few crumbs that were scattered about, she ran back into the wall and scrambled up to her nest.

Hickory and Dickory and Dock were very glad to get the crumbs, for they were hungry; and when they had breakfasted they all curled up alongside their mother and slept soundly throughout the day.

"Be good children," said Mamma Mouse the next evening, as she prepared for her journey to the pantry, "and do n't stir out of your nest till I come back. I am in hopes that after to-night we shall not be hungry for a long time, as I shall gnaw a hole at the back of the flour barrel, where it will not be discovered."

She kissed each one of them good-bye and ran down the wall on her errand.

When they were left alone Hickory wanted to go to sleep again, but little Dock was wide awake, and tumbled around so in the nest that his brothers were unable to sleep.

"I wish I could go with mother some night," said Dock, "it 's no fun to stay here all the time."

"She will take us when we are big enough," replied Dickory.

"We are big enough now," declared Dock, "and if I knew my way I would go out into the world and see what it looks like."

"I know a way out," said Hickory, "but mamma would n't like it if we should go without her permission."

"She need n't know anything about it," declared the naughty Dock, "for she will be busy at the flour-barrel all the night. Take us out for a little walk, Hick, if you know the way."

"Yes do," urged Dickory.

"Well," said Hickory, "I 'd like a little stroll myself, so if you 'll promise to be very careful, and not get into any mischief, I 'll take you through the hole that I have discovered."

So the three little mice started off, with Hickory showing the way, and soon came to a crack in the wall. Hickory stuck his head through, and finding everything quiet, for the family of people that lived in the house were fast asleep, he squeezed through the crack, followed by his two brothers. Their little hearts beat very fast, for they knew if they were discovered they would have to run for their lives; but the house was so still they gained courage, and crept along over a thick carpet until they came to a stairway.

"What shall we do now?" whispered Hickory to his brothers.

"Let 's go down," replied Dock.

So, very carefully, they descended the stairs and reached the hallway of the house, and here they were much surprised by all they saw.

There was a big rack for hats and coats, and an umbrella stand, and two quaintly carved chairs, and, most wonderful of all, a tall clock that stood upon the floor and ticked out the minutes in a grave and solemn voice.

When the little mice first heard the ticking of the clock they were inclined to be frightened, and huddled close together upon the bottom stair.

"What is it?" asked Dickory, in an awed whisper.

"I do n't know," replied Hickory, who was himself rather afraid.

"Is it alive?" asked Dock.

"I do n't know," again answered Hickory.

Then, seeing that the clock paid no attention to them, but kept ticking steadily away and seemed to mind its own business, they plucked up courage and began running about.

Presently Dickory uttered a delighted squeal that brought his brothers to his side. There in a corner lay nearly the half of a bun which little May had dropped when nurse carried her upstairs to bed. It was a great discovery for the three mice, and they ate heartily until the last crumb had disappeared.

"This is better than a cupboard or a pantry," said Dock, when they had finished their supper, "and I should n't be surprised if there were plenty more good things around if we only hunt for them."

But they could find nothing more, for all the doors leading into the hall were closed, and at last Dock came to the clock and looked at it curiously.

"It does n't seem to be alive," he thought, "although it does make so much noise. I 'm going behind it to see what I can find."

He found nothing except a hole that led to the inside of the clock, and into this he stuck his head. He could hear the ticking plainer than ever now, but looking way up to the top of the clock he saw something shining brightly, and thought it must be good to eat if he could only get at it. Without saying anything to his brothers, Dock ran up the sides of the clock until he came to the works, and he was just about to nibble at a glistening wheel, to see what it tasted like, when suddenly "Bang!" went the clock.

It was one o'clock, and the clock had only struck the hour, but the great gong was just beside Dock's ear and the noise nearly deafened the poor little mouse. He gave a scream of terror and ran down the clock as fast as he could go. When he reached the hall he heard his brothers scampering up the stairs, and after them he ran with all his might.

It was only when they were safe in their nest again that they stopped to breathe, and their little hearts beat fast for an hour afterward, so great had been their terror.

When Mamma Mouse came back in the morning, bringing a quantity of nice flour with her for breakfast, they told her of their adventure.

She thought they had been punished enough already for their disobedience, so she did not scold them, but only said,

"You see, my dears, your mother knew best when she told you not to stir from the nest. Children sometimes think they know more than their parents, but this adventure should teach you always to obey your mother. The next time you run away you may fare worse than you did last night; remember your poor father's fate."

But Hickory and Dickory and Dock did not run away again.

Little Bo-Peep

Little Bo-Peep

ON the beautiful, undulating hills of Sussex feed many flocks of sheep, which are tended by many shepherds and shepherdesses, and one of these flocks used to be cared for by a poor woman who supported herself and her little girl by this means.

They lived in a small cottage nestled at the foot of one of the hills, and each morning the mother took her crook and started out with her sheep, that they might feed upon the tender, juicy grasses with which the hills abounded. The little girl usually accompanied her mother and sat by her side upon the grassy mounds and watched her care for the ewes and lambs, so that in time she herself grew to be a very proficient shepherdess.

So when the mother became too old and feeble to leave her cottage, Little Bo-Peep (as she was called) decided that she was fully able to manage the flocks herself. She was a little mite of a child, with flowing nut-brown locks and big gray eyes that charmed all who gazed into their innocent depths. She wore a light gray frock, fastened about the waist with a pretty pink sash, and there were white ruffles around her neck and pink ribbons in her hair.

All the shepherds and shepherdesses upon the hills, both young and old, soon came to know Little Bo-Peep very well indeed, and there were many willing hands to aid her if (which was not often) she needed their assistance.

Bo-Peep usually took her sheep to the side of a high hill above the cottage, and allowed them to eat the rich grass while she herself sat upon a mound and, laying aside her crook and her broad straw hat with its pink ribbons, devoted her time to sewing and mending stockings for her aged mother.

One day, while thus occupied, she heard a voice beside her say:

"Good morning, Little Bo-Peep!" and looking up the girl saw a woman standing near her and leaning upon a short stick. She was bent nearly double by weight of many years, her hair was white as snow and her eyes as black as coals. Deep wrinkles seamed her face and hands, while her nose and chin were so pointed that they nearly met. She was not pleasant to look upon, but Bo-Peep had learned to be polite to the aged, so she answered, sweetly,

"Good morning, mother. Can I do anything for you?"

"No, dearie," returned the woman, in a cracked voice, "but I will sit by your side and rest for a time."

The girl made room on the mound beside her, and the stranger sat down and watched in silence the busy fingers sew up the seams of the new frock she was making.

By and by the woman asked,

"Why do you come out here to sew?"

"Because I am a shepherdess," replied the girl.

"But where is your crook?"

"On the grass beside me."

"And where are your sheep?"

Bo-Peep looked up and could not see them.

"They must have strayed over the top of the hill," she said, "and I will go and seek them."

"Do not be in a hurry," croaked the old woman; "they will return presently without your troubling to find them."

"Do you think so?" asked Bo-Peep.

"Of course; do not the sheep know you?"

"Oh, yes; they know me every one."

"And do not you know the sheep?"

"I can call every one by name," said Bo-Peep, confidently; "for though I am so young a shepherdess I am fond of my sheep and know all about them."

The old woman chuckled softly, as if the answer amused her, and replied,

"No one knows all about anything, my dear."

"But I know all about my sheep," protested Little Bo-Peep.

"Do you, indeed? Then you are wiser that most people. And if you know all about them, you also know they will come home of their own accord, and

I have no doubt they will all be wagging their tails behind them, as usual."

"Oh," said Little Bo-Peep, in surprise, "do they wag their tails? I never noticed that!"

"Indeed!" excaimed the old woman, "then you are not very observing for one who knows all about sheep. Perhaps you have never noticed their tails at all."

"No," answered Bo-Peep, thoughtfully, "I do n't know that I ever have."

The woman laughed so hard at this reply that she began to cough, and this made the girl remember that her flock had strayed away.

"I really must go and find my sheep," she said, rising to her feet, "and then I shall be sure to notice their tails, and see if they wag them."

"Sit still, my child," said the old woman, "I am going over the hill-top myself, and I will send the sheep back to you."

So she got upon her feet and began climbing the hill, and the girl heard her saying, as she walked away,

"Little Bo-Peep has lost her sheep,
  And does n't know where to find 'em.
But leave 'em alone, and they 'll come home,
  All wagging their tails behind 'em."

Little Bo-Peep sat still and watched the old woman toil slowly up the hill-side and disappear over the top. By and by she thought, "very soon I shall see the sheep coming back;" but time passed away and still the errant flock failed to make its appearance.

Soon the head of the little shepherdess began to nod, and presently, still thinking of her sheep,

> Little Bo-Peep fell fast asleep,
> And dreamt she heard them bleating;
> But when she awoke she found it a joke,
> For still they wère a-fleeting.

The girl now became quite anxious, and wondered why the old woman had not driven her flock over the hill. But as it was now time for luncheon she opened her little basket and ate of the bread and cheese and cookies she had brought with her. After she had finished her meal and taken a drink of cool water from a spring near by, she decided she would not wait any longer.

> So up she took her little crook,
> Determined for to find them,

and began climbing the hill.

When she got to the top there was never a sight of sheep about—only a green valley and another hill beyond.

Now really alarmed for the safety of her charge, Bo-Peep hurried into the valley and up the farther hill-side. Panting and tired she reached the summit, and, pausing breathlessly, gazed below her.

Quietly feeding upon the rich grass was her truant

flock, looking as peaceful and innocent as if it had never strayed away from its gentle shepherdess.

Bo-Peep uttered a cry of joy and hurried toward them; but when she came near she stopped in amazement and held up her little hands with a pretty expression of dismay. She had

> Found them, indeed, but it made her heart bleed,
> For they 'd left their tails behind them!

Nothing was left to each sheep but a wee little stump where a tail should be, and Little Bo-Peep was so heart-broken that she sat down beside them and sobbed bitterly.

But after awhile the tiny maid realized that all her tears would not bring back the tails to her lambkins; so she plucked up courage and dried her eyes and arose from the ground just as the old woman hobbled up to her.

"So you have found your sheep, dearie," she said, in her cracked voice.

"Yes," replied Little Bo-Peep, with difficulty repressing a sob; "but look, mother! They 've all left their tails behind them!"

"Why, so they have!" exclaimed the old woman; and then she began to laugh as if something pleased her.

"What do you suppose has become of their tails?" asked the girl.

"Oh, some one has probably cut them off. They

Little Bo-Peep

make nice tippets in winter-time, you know;" and then she patted the child upon her head and walked away down the valley.

Bo-Peep was much grieved over the loss that had befallen her dear sheep, and so, driving them before her, she wandered around to see if by any chance she could find the lost tails.

But soon the sun began to sink over the hill-tops, and she knew she must take her sheep home before night overtook them.

She did not tell her mother of her misfortune, for she feared the old shepherdess would scold her, and Bo-Peep had fully decided to seek for the tails and find them before she related the story of their loss to any one.

Each day for many days after that Little Bo-Peep wandered about the hills seeking the tails of her sheep, and those who met her wondered what had happened to make the sweet little maid so anxious. But there is an end to all troubles, no matter how severe they may seem to be, and

> It happened one day, as Bo-Peep did stray
> Unto a meadow hard by,
> There she espied their tails side by side,
> All hung on a tree to dry!

The little shepherdess was overjoyed at this discovery, and, reaching up her crook, she knocked the row of pretty white tails off the tree and gathered them up in her frock. But how to fasten them onto her sheep again was the question, and after pondering the matter for a time she became discouraged, and, thinking she was no better off than before the tails were found, she began to weep and to bewail her misfortune.

But amidst her tears she bethought herself of her needle and thread.

"Why," she exclaimed, smiling again, "I can sew them on, of course!" Then

She heaved a sigh and wiped her eye
And ran o'er hill and dale, oh,
  And tried what she could
  As a shepherdess should,
To tack to each sheep its tail, oh.

But the very first sheep she came to refused to allow her to sew on the tail, and ran away from her, and the others did the same, so that finally she was utterly discouraged.

She was beginning to cry again, when the same old woman she had before met came hobbling to her side and asked,

"What are you doing with my cat tails?"

"Your cat tails!" replied Bo-Peep, in surprise; "what do you mean?"

"Why, these tails are all cut from white pussy-cats, and I put them on the tree to dry. What are you doing with them?"

"I thought they belonged to my sheep," answered Bo-Peep, sorrowfully; "but if they are really your pussy-cat tails, I must hunt until I find those that belong to my sheep."

"My dear," said the old woman, "I have been deceiving you; you said you knew all about your sheep, and I wanted to teach you a lesson. For, however wise we may be, no one in this world knows *all* about anything. Sheep do not have long tails—there is only a little stump to answer for a tail. Neither do rabbits have tails, nor bears, nor many other animals. And if you had been observing you would have known all this when I said the sheep would be wagging their tails behind them, and then you would not have passed all those days in searching for what is not to be found. So now, little one, run away home, and try to be more thoughtful in the future. Your sheep will never miss the tails, for they have never had them."

And now

Little Bo-Peep no more did weep;
My tale of tails ends here.
Each cat has one,
But sheep have none;
Which, after all, is queer!

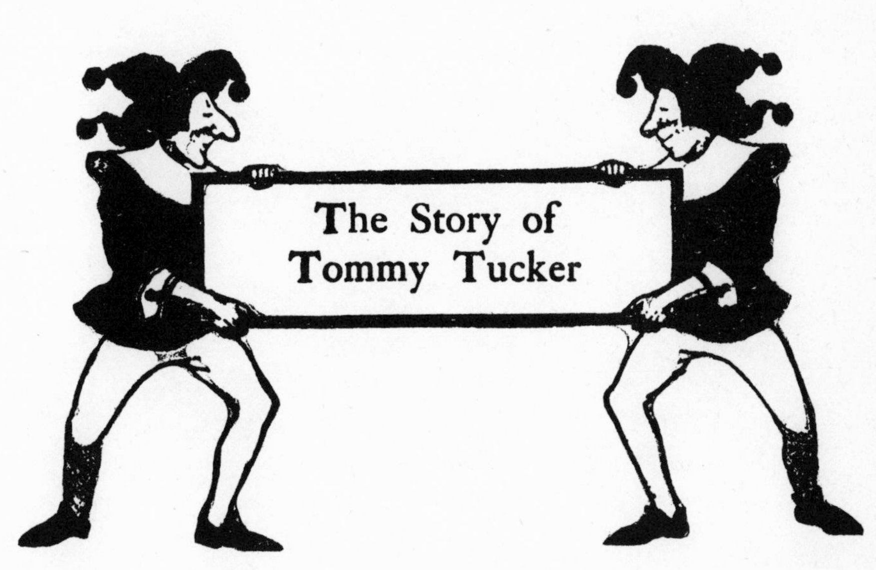
The Story of
Tommy Tucker

The Story of Tommy Tucker

Little Tommy Tucker sang for his supper.
What did he sing for? white bread and butter.
How could he cut it, without any knife?
How could he marry, without any wife?

LITTLE TOMMY TUCKER was a waif of the streets. He never remembered having a father or mother or any one to care for him, and so he learned to care for himself. He ate whatever he could get, and slept wherever night overtook him—in an old barrel, a cellar, or, when fortune favored him, he paid a penny for a cot in some rude lodging-house.

His life about the streets taught him early how to earn a living by doing odd jobs, and he learned to be sharp in his speech and wise beyond his years.

One morning Tommy crawled out from a box in which he had slept over night, and found that he was hungry. His last meal had consisted of a crust of bread, and he was a growing boy with an appetite.

He had been unable to earn any money for several days, and this morning life looked very gloomy to him. He started out to seek for work or to beg a breakfast; but luck was against him, and he was unsuccessful. By noon he had grown more hungry than before, and stood before a bake-shop for a long time, looking wistfully at the good things behind the window-panes, and wishing with all his heart he had a ha'penny to buy a bun.

And yet it was no new thing for Little Tommy Tucker to be hungry, and he never thought of despairing. He sat down upon a curb-stone, and thought what was best to be done. Then he remembered he had frequently begged a meal at one of the cottages that stood upon the outskirts of the city, and so he turned his steps in that direction.

"I have had neither breakfast nor dinner," he said to himself, "and I must surely find a supper somewhere, or I shall not sleep much to-night. It is no fun to be hungry."

So he walked on until he came to a dwelling-house where a goodly company sat upon a lawn and beneath a veranda. It was a pretty place, and was the home of a fat alderman who had been married that very day.

The alderman was in a merry mood, and seeing Tommy standing without the gate he cried to him,

"Come here, my lad, and sing us a song."

Tommy at once entered the grounds, and came to where the fat alderman was sitting beside his blushing bride.

"Can you sing?" enquired the alderman.

"No," answered Tommy, earnestly, "but I can eat."

"Ho, ho!" laughed the alderman, "that is a very ordinary accomplishment. Anyone can eat."

"If it please you, sir, you are wrong," replied Tommy, "for I have been unable to eat all day."

"And why is that?" asked the alderman.

"Because I have had nothing to put to my mouth. But now that I have met so kind a gentleman, I am sure that I shall have a good supper."

The alderman laughed again at this shrewd answer, and said,

"You shall have supper, no doubt; but you must sing a song for the company first, and so earn your food."

Tommy shook his head sadly.

"I do not know any song, sir," he said.

The alderman called a servant and whispered something in his ear. The servant hastened away, and soon returned bearing upon a tray a huge slice of white bread and butter. White bread was a rare treat in those days, as nearly all the people ate black bread baked from rye or barley flour.

"Now," said the alderman, placing the tray beside him, "you shall have this slice of white bread and butter when you have sung us a song, and complied with one condition."

"And what is that condition?" asked Tommy.

"I will tell you when we have heard the song," replied the fat alderman, who had decided to have some amusement at the boy's expense.

Tommy hesitated, but when he glanced at the white bread and butter his mouth watered in spite of himself, and he resolved to compose a song, since he did not know how to sing any other.

So he took off his cap, and standing before the company he sang as follows:

"A bumble-bee lit on a hollyhock flower
That was wet with the rain of a morning shower.
While the honey he sipped
His left foot slipped,
And he could n't fly again for half an hour!"

"Good!" cried the alderman, after the company had kindly applauded Tommy. "I can't say much for the air, nor yet for the words; but it was not so bad as it might have been. Give us another verse."

So Tommy pondered a moment, and then sang again:

"A spider threw its web so high
It caught on a moon in a cloudy sky.
The moon whirled round,
And down to the ground
Fell the web, and captured a big blue fly!"

"Why, that is fine!" roared the fat alderman. "You improve as you go on, so give us another verse."

"I don't know any more," said Tommy, "and I am very hungry."

"One more verse," persisted the man, "and then you shall have the bread and butter upon the condition."

So Tommy sang the following verse:

Tommy Tucker

"A big frog lived in a slimy bog,
And caught a cold in an awful fog.
The cold got worse,
The frog got hoarse,
Till croaking he scared a polliwog!"

"You are quite a poet," declared the alderman; "and now you shall have the white bread upon one condition."

"What is it?" said Tommy, anxiously.

"That you cut the slice into four parts."

"But I have no knife!" remonstrated the boy.

"But that is the condition," insisted the alderman. "If you want the bread you must cut it."

"Surely you do not expect me to cut the bread without any knife!" said Tommy.

"Why not?" asked the alderman, winking his eye at the company.

"Because it cannot be done. How, let me ask you, sir, could you have married without any wife?"

"Ha, ha, ha!" laughed the jolly alderman; and he was so pleased with Tommy's apt reply that he gave him the bread at once, and a knife to cut it with.

"Thank you, sir," said Tommy; "now that I have the knife it is easy enough to cut the bread, and I shall now be as happy as you are with your beautiful wife."

The alderman's wife blushed at this, and whispered to her husband. The alderman nodded in reply, and watched Tommy carefully as he ate his supper. When the boy had finished his bread—which he did very quickly, you may be sure,—the man said,

"How would you like to live with me and be my servant?"

Little Tommy Tucker had often longed for just such a place, where he could have three meals each day to eat and a good bed to sleep in at night, so he answered,

"I should like it very much, sir."

So the alderman took Tommy for his servant, and dressed him in a smart livery; and soon the boy showed by his bright ways and obedience that he was worthy any kindness bestowed upon him.

He often carried the alderman's wig when his master attended the town meetings, and the mayor of the city, who was a good man, was much taken with his intelligent face. So one day he said to the alderman,

"I have long wanted to adopt a son, for I have no children of my own; but I have not yet been able to find a boy to suit me. That lad of yours looks bright and intelligent, and he seems a well-behaved boy into the bargain."

"He is all that you say," returned the alderman, "and would be a credit to you should you adopt him."

"But before I adopt a son," continued the mayor, "I intend to satisfy myself that he is both wise and shrewd enough to make good use of my money when

I am gone. No fool will serve my purpose; therefore I shall test the boy's wit before I decide."

"That is fair enough," answered the alderman; "but in what way will you test his wit?"

"Bring him to my house to-morrow, and you shall see," said the mayor.

So the next day the alderman, followed by Tommy and a little terrier dog that was a great pet of his master, went to the grand dwelling of the mayor. The mayor also had a little terrier dog, which was very fond of him and followed him wherever he went.

When Tommy and the alderman reached the mayor's house the mayor met them at the door and said:

"Tommy, I am going up the street, and the alderman is going in the opposite direction. I want you to keep our dogs from following us; but you must not do it by holding them."

"Very well, sir," replied Tommy; and as the mayor started one way and the alderman the other, he took out his handkerchief and tied the tails of the two dogs together. Of course each dog started to follow its master; but as they were about the same size and strength, and each pulled in a different direction, the result was that they remained in one place, and could not move either one way or the other.

"That was well done," said the mayor, coming back again; "but tell me, can you put my cart before my horse and take me to ride?"

"Certainly, sir," replied Tommy; and going to the mayor's stable he put the harness on the nag and then led him head-first into the shafts, instead of backing him into them, as is the usual way. After fastening the shafts to the horse, he mounted upon the animal's back, and away they started, pushing the cart before the horse.

"That was easy," said Tommy. "If your honor will get into the cart I'll take you to ride." But the mayor did not ride, although he was pleased at Tommy's readiness in solving a difficulty.

After a moment's thought he bade Tommy follow him into the house, where he gave him a cupful of water, saying,

"Let me see you drink up this cup of water."

Tommy hesitated a moment, for he knew the mayor was trying to catch him; then, going to a corner of the room, he set down the cup and stood upon his head in the corner. He now carefully raised the cup to his lips and slowly drank the water until the cup was empty. After this he regained his feet, and, bowing politely to the mayor, he said,

"The water is drunk up, your honor."

"But why did you stand on your head to do it?" enquired the alderman, who had watched the act in astonishment.

"Because otherwise I would have drunk the water down, and not up," replied Tommy.

The mayor was now satisfied that Tommy was

shrewd enough to do him honor, so he immediately took him to live in the great house as his adopted son, and he was educated by the best masters the city afforded.

And Tommy Tucker became in after years not only a great, but a good man, and before he died was himself mayor of the city, and was known by the name of Sir Thomas Tucker.

Pussy-cat Mew

Pussy-cat Mew

"Pussy-cat, Pussy-cat, where do you go?"
"To London, to visit the palace, you know."
"Pussy-cat Mew, will you come back again?"
"Oh, yes! I'll scamper with might and with main!"

PUSSY-CAT MEW set off on her way, *Pussy-cat Mew*
Stepping quite softly and feeling quite gay.
Smooth was the road, so she traveled at ease,
Warmed by the sunshine and fanned by the breeze.

Over the hills to the valleys below,
Through the deep woods where the soft mosses grow,
Skirting the fields, with buttercups dotted,
Swiftly our venturesome Pussy-cat trotted.

Sharp watch she kept when a village she neared,
For boys and their mischief our Pussy-cat feared.
Often she crept through the grasses so deep
To pass by a dog that was lying asleep.

Once, as she walked through a sweet-clover field,
Something beside her affrightedly squealed,
And swift from her path there darted away
A tiny field-mouse, with a coat of soft gray.

"Now here," thought our Pussy, "is chance for a dinner;
The one that runs fastest must surely be winner!"
So quickly she started the mouse to give chase,
And over the clover they ran a great race.

But just when it seemed that Pussy would win,
The mouse spied a hole and quickly popped in;
And so he escaped, for the hole was so small
That Pussy-cat could n't squeeze in it at all.

So, softly she crouched, and with eyes big and round
Quite steadily watched that small hole in the ground.
"This mouse really thinks he 's escaped me," she said,
"But I 'll catch him sure if he sticks out his head!"

But while she was watching the poor mouse's plight,
A deep growl behind made her jump with affright;
She gave a great cry, and then started to run
As swift as a bullet that 's shot from a gun!

"Meow! Oh, meow!" our poor Puss did say;
"Bow-wow!" cried the dog, who was not far away.
O'er meadows and ditches they scampered apace,
O'er fences and hedges they kept up the race!

Then Pussy-cat Mew saw before her a tree,
And knew that a safe place of refuge 't would be;
So far up the tree with a bound she did go,
And left the big dog to growl down below.

But now, by good fortune, a man came that way,
And called to the dog, who was forced to obey;
But Puss did not come down the tree till she knew
That the man and the dog were far out of view.

Pursuing her way, at nightfall she came
To London, a town you know well by name;
And wandering 'round in byway and street,
A strange Pussy-cat she happened to meet.

"Good evening," said Pussy-cat Mew. "Can you tell
In which of these houses the Queen may now dwell?
I'm a stranger in town, and I'm anxious to see
What sort of a person a real Queen may be."

"My friend," said the other, "you really must know
It isn't permitted that strangers should go
Inside of the palace, unless they're invited,
And stray Pussy-cats are apt to be slighted.

"By good luck, however, I'm quite well aware
Of a way to the palace by means of a stair
That never is guarded; so just come with me,
And a glimpse of the Queen you shall certainly see."

Puss thanked her new friend, and together they stole
To the back of the palace, and crept through a hole
In the fence, and quietly came to the stair
Which the stranger Pussy-cat promised was there.

"Now here I must leave you," the strange Pussy said,
"So do n't be 'fraid-cat, but go straight ahead,
And do n't be alarmed if by chance you are seen,
For people will think you belong to the Queen."

So Pussy-cat Mew did as she had been told,
And walked through the palace with manner so bold
She soon reached the room where the Queen sat in state,
Surrounded by lords and by ladies so great.

And there in the corner our Pussy sat down,
And gazed at the scepter and blinked at the crown,
And eyed the Queen's dress, all purple and gold;
Which was surely a beautiful sight to behold.

But all of a sudden she started, for there
Was a little gray mouse, right under the chair
Where her Majesty sat, and Pussy well knew
She 'd scream with alarm if the mouse met her view.

So up toward the chair our Pussy-cat stole,
But the mouse saw her coming and ran for its hole;
But Pussy ran after, and during the race
A wonderful, terrible panic took place!

The ladies all jumped on their chairs in alarm,
The lords drew their swords to protect them from harm,
And the Queen gave a scream and fainted away—
A very undignified act, I must say.

And some one cried "Burglars!" and some one cried
"Treason!"
And some one cried "Murder!" but none knew the
reason;
And some one cried "Fire! they are burning the house!"
And some one cried "Silence! it's only a mouse!"

But Pussy-cat Mew was so awfully scared
By the shouting and screaming, no longer she dared
To stay in the room; so without more delay
She rushed from the palace and scampered away!

So bristling her fur, and with heart beating fast,
She came to the road leading homeward at last.
"What business," she thought, "has a poor country cat
To visit a city of madmen like that?

"Straight homeward I'll go, where I am well fed,
Where mistress is kind, and soft is my bed;
Let other cats travel, if they wish to roam,
But as for myself, I shall now stay at home."

And now over hills and valleys she ran,
And journeyed as fast as a Pussy-cat can;
Till just as the dawn of the day did begin
She, safely at home, stole quietly in.

And there was the fire, with the pot boiling on it,
And there was the maid, in the blue checkered bonnet,
And there was the corner where Pussy oft basked,
And there was the mistress, who eagerly asked:

"*Pussy-cat, Pussy-cat, where have you been?*"
"*I've been to London, to visit the Queen.*"
"*Pussy-cat, Pussy-cat, what did you there?*"
"*I frightened a little mouse under her chair!*"

How the Beggars
Came to Town

How the Beggars Came to Town

Hark, hark, the dogs do bark,
The beggars are coming to town:
Some in rags, and some in tags,
And some in velvet gown.

VERY fair and sweet was little Prince Lilimond, and few could resist his soft, pleading voice and gentle blue eyes. And as he stood in the presence of the King, his father, and bent his knee gracefully before His Majesty, the act was so courteous and dignified it would have honored the oldest nobleman of the court.

The King was delighted, and for a time sat silently regarding his son and noting every detail of his appearance, from the dark velvet suit with its dainty ruffles and collar to the diamond buckles on the little shoes, and back again to the flowing curls that clustered thick about the bright, childish face.

Well might any father be proud of so manly and beautiful a child, and the King's heart swelled within him as he gazed upon his heir.

"Borland," he said to the tutor, who stood modestly behind the Prince, "you may retire. I wish to speak privately with his royal highness."

The tutor bowed low and disappeared within the ante-room, and the King continued, kindly,

"Come here, Lilimond, and sit beside me. Methinks you seem over-grave this morning."

"It is my birthday, Your Majesty," replied the Prince, as he slowly obeyed his father and sat beside him upon the rich broidered cushions of the throne. "I am twelve years of age."

"So old!" said the King, smiling into the little face that was raised to his. "And is it the weight of years that makes you sad?"

"No, Your Majesty; I long for the years to pass, that I may become a man, and take my part in the world's affairs. It is the sad condition of my country which troubles me."

"Indeed!" exclaimed the King, casting a keen glance at his son. "Are you becoming interested in politics, then; or is there some grievous breach of court etiquette which has attracted your attention?"

"I know little of politics and less of the court, sire," replied Lilimond; "it is the distress of the people that worries me."

"The people? Of a surety, Prince, you are better posted than am I, since of the people and their affairs I know nothing at all. I have appointed officers to look after their interests, and therefore I have no cause to come into contact with them myself. But what is amiss?"

"They are starving," said the Prince, looking at his

father very seriously; "the country is filled with beggars, who appeal for charity, since they are unable otherwise to procure food."

"Starving!" repeated the King; "surely you are misinformed. My Lord Chamberlain told me but this morning the people were loyal and contented, and my Lord of the Treasury reports that all taxes and tithes have been paid, and my coffers are running over."

"Your Lord Chamberlain is wrong, sire," returned the Prince; "my tutor, Borland, and I have talked with many of these beggars the past few days, and we find the tithes and taxes which have enriched you have taken the bread from their wives and children."

"So!" exclaimed the King. "We must examine into this matter." He touched a bell beside him, and when a retainer appeared directed his Chamberlain and his Treasurer to wait upon him at once.

The Prince rested his head upon his hand and waited patiently, but the King was very impatient indeed till the high officers of the court stood before him. Then said the King, addressing his Chamberlain,

"Sir, I am informed my people are murmuring at my injustice. Is it true?"

The officer cast an enquiring glance at the Prince, who met his eyes gravely, before he replied,

"The people always murmur, Your Majesty. They are many, and not all can be content, even when ruled by so wise and just a King. In every land and in every age there are those who rebel against the laws, and the protests of the few are ever heard above the contentment of the many."

"I am told," continued the King, severely, "that my country is overrun with beggars, who suffer for lack of the bread we have taken from them by our taxations. Is this true?"

"There are always beggars, Your Majesty, in every country," replied the Chamberlain, "and it is their custom to blame others for their own misfortunes."

The King thought deeply for a moment; then he turned to the Lord of the Treasury.

"Do we tax the poor?" he demanded.

"All are taxed, sire," returned the Treasurer, who was pale from anxiety, for never before had the King so questioned him, "but from the rich we take much, from the poor very little."

"But a little from the poor man may distress him, while the rich subject would never feel the loss. Why do we tax the poor at all?"

"Because, Your Majesty, should we declare the poor free from taxation all your subjects would at once claim to be poor, and the royal treasury would remain empty. And as none are so rich but there are those richer, how should we, in justice, determine which are the rich and which are the poor?"

Again the King was silent while he pondered upon the words of the Royal Treasurer. Then, with a wave of his hand, he dismissed them, and turned to the Prince, saying,

"You have heard the wise words of my councilors, Prince. What have you to say in reply?"

"If you will pardon me, Your Majesty, I think you are wrong to leave the affairs of the people to others to direct. If you knew them as well as I do, you would distrust the words of your councilors, who naturally fear your anger more than they do that of your subjects."

"If they fear my anger they will be careful to do no injustice to my people. Surely you cannot expect me to attend to levying the taxes myself," continued the King, with growing annoyance. "What are my officers for, but to serve me?"

"They should serve you, it is true," replied the Prince, thoughtfully, "but they should serve the people as well."

"Nonsense!" answered the King; "you are too young as yet to properly understand such matters. And it is a way youth has to imagine it is wiser than age and experience combined. Still, I will investigate the subject further, and see that justice is done the poor."

"In the meantime," said the Prince, "many will starve to death. Can you not assist these poor beggars at once?"

"In what way?" demanded the King.

"By giving them money from your full coffers."

"Nonsense!" again cried the King, this time with real anger; "you have heard what the Chamberlain said: we always have beggars, and none, as yet, have starved to death. Besides, I must use the money for the grand ball and tourney next month, as I have promised the ladies of the court a carnival of unusual magnificence."

The Prince did not reply to this, but remained in silent thought, wondering what he might do to ease the suffering he feared existed on every hand amongst the poor of the kingdom. He had hoped to persuade the King to assist these beggars, but since the interview with the officers of the court he had lost heart and despaired of influencing his royal father in any way.

Suddenly the King spoke.

"Let us dismiss this subject, Lilimond, for it only serves to distress us both, and no good can come of it. You have nearly made me forget it is your birthday. Now listen, my son: I am much pleased with you, and thank God that he has given me such a successor for my crown, for I perceive your mind is as beautiful as your person, and that you will in time be fitted to rule the land with wisdom and justice. Therefore I promise, in honor of your birthday, to grant any desire you may express, provided it lies within my power. Nor will I make any further condition, since I rely upon your judgment to select some gift I may be glad to bestow."

As the King spoke, Lilimond suddenly became impressed with an idea through which he might succor the poor, and therefore he answered,

"Call in the ladies and gentlemen of the court, my father, and before them all will I claim your promise."

"Good!" exclaimed the King, who looked for some amusement in his son's request; and at once he ordered the court to assemble.

The ladies and gentlemen, as they filed into the audience chamber, were astonished to see the Prince seated upon the throne beside his sire, but being too well bred to betray their surprise they only wondered what amusement His Majesty had in store for them.

When all were assembled, the Prince rose to his feet and addressed them.

"His Majesty the King, whose kindness of heart and royal condescension is well known to you all, hath but now promised me, seeing that it is my birthday, to grant any one request that I may prefer. Is it not true, Your Majesty?"

"It is true," answered the King, smiling upon his son, and pleased to see him addressing the court so gravely and with so manly an air; "whatsoever the Prince may ask, that will I freely grant."

"Then, oh sire," said the Prince, kneeling before the throne, "I ask that for the period of one day I may reign as King in your stead, having at my command all kingly power and the obedience of all who owe allegiance to the crown!"

For a time there was perfect silence in the court, the King growing red with dismay and embarrassment and the courtiers waiting curiously his reply. Lilimond still remained kneeling before the throne, and as the King looked upon him he realized it would be impossible to break his royal word. And the affair promised him amusement after all, so he quickly decided in what manner to reply.

"Rise, oh Prince," he said, cheerfully, "your request is granted. Upon what day will it please you to reign?"

Lilimond arose to his feet.

"Upon the seventh day from this," he answered.

"So be it," returned the King. Then, turning to the royal herald he added, "Make proclamation throughout the kingdom that on the seventh day from this Prince Lilimond will reign as King from sunrise till sunset. And whoever dares to disobey his commands will be guilty of treason and shall be punished with death!"

The court was then dismissed, all wondering at this marvellous decree, and the Prince returned to his own apartment where his tutor, Borland, anxiously awaited him.

Now this Borland was a man of good heart and much intelligence, but wholly unused to the ways of the world. He had lately noted, with much grief, the number of beggars who solicited alms as he walked out with the Prince, and he had given freely until his purse was empty. Then he talked long and earnestly with the Prince concerning this shocking condition in the kingdom, never dreaming that his own generosity had attracted all the beggars of the city toward him and encouraged them to become more bold than usual.

Thus was the young and tender-hearted Prince brought to a knowledge of all these beggars, and therefore it was that their condition filled him with sadness and induced him to speak so boldly to the King, his father.

When he returned to Borland with the tidings that the King had granted him permission to rule for a day the kingdom, the tutor was overjoyed, and at once they began to plan ways for relieving all the poor of the country in that one day.

For one thing, they dispatched private messengers to every part of the kingdom, bidding them tell each beggar they met to come to the Prince on that one day he should be King and he would relieve their wants, giving a broad gold piece to every poor man or woman who asked.

For the Prince had determined to devote to this purpose the gold that filled the royal coffers; and as for the great ball and tourney the King had planned, why, that could go begging much better than the starving people.

On the night before the day the Prince was to reign there was a great confusion of noise within the city, for beggars from all parts of the kingdom began to arrive, each one filled with joy at the prospect of receiving a piece of gold.

There was a continual tramp, tramp of feet, and a great barking of dogs, as all dogs in those days were trained to bark at every beggar they saw, and now it was difficult to restrain them.

And the beggars came to town singly and by twos and threes, until hundreds were there to await the morrow. Some few were very pitiful to behold, being feeble and infirm from age and disease, dressed in rags and tags, and presenting an appearance of great distress. But there were many more who were seemingly hearty and vigorous; and these were the lazy ones, who, not being willing to work, begged for a livelihood.

And some there were dressed in silken hose and velvet gowns, who, forgetting all shame, and, eager for gold, had been led by the Prince's offer to represent themselves as beggars, that they might add to their wealth without trouble or cost to themselves.

The next morning, when the sun arose upon the eventful day, it found the Prince sitting upon the throne of his father, dressed in a robe of ermine and purple, a crown upon his flowing locks and the King's scepter clasped tightly in his little hand. He was somewhat frightened at the clamor of the crowd without the palace, but Borland, who stood behind him, whispered,

"The more you can succor the greater will be your glory, and you will live in the hearts of your people as the kind Prince who relieved their sufferings. Be of good cheer, Your Majesty, for all is well."

Then did the Prince command the Treasurer to bring before him the royal coffers, and to stand ready to present to each beggar a piece of gold. The Treasurer was very unwilling to do this, but he was under penalty of death if he refused, and so the coffers were brought forth.

"Your Majesty," said the Treasurer, "if each of those who clamor without is to receive a piece of gold, there will not be enough within these coffers to go around. Some will receive and others be denied, since no further store of gold is to be had."

At this news the Prince was both puzzled and alarmed.

"What are we to do?" he asked of the tutor; but Borland was unable to suggest a remedy.

Then said the aged Chamberlain, coming forward, and bowing low before the little King,

"Your Majesty, I think I can assist you in your difficulty. You did but promise a piece of gold to those who are really suffering and in need, but so great is the greed of mankind that many without are in no necessity whatever, but only seek to enrich themselves at your expense. Therefore I propose you examine carefully each case that presents itself, and unless the beggar is in need of alms turn him away empty-handed, as being a fraud and a charlatan."

"Your counsel is wise, oh Chamberlain," replied

the Prince, after a moment's thought; "and by turning away the impostors we shall have gold enough for the needy. Therefore bid the guards to admit the beggars one by one."

When the first beggar came before him the Prince asked,

"Are you in need?"

"I am starving, Your Majesty," replied the man, in a whining tone. He was poorly dressed, but seemed strong and well, and the Prince examined him carefully for a moment. Then he answered the fellow, saying,

"Since you are starving, go and sell the gold ring I see you are wearing upon your finger. I can assist only those who are unable to help themselves."

At this the man turned away muttering angrily, and the courtiers murmured their approval of the Prince's wisdom.

The next beggar was dressed in velvet, and the Prince sent him away with a sharp rebuke. But the third was a woman, old and feeble, and she blessed the Prince as she hobbled joyfully away with a broad gold-piece clasped tightly within her withered hand.

The next told so pitiful a story that he also received a gold-piece; but as he turned away the Prince saw that beneath his robe his shoes were fastened with silver buckles, and so he commanded the guards to take away the gold and to punish the man for attempting to deceive his King.

And so many came to him that were found to be unworthy that he finally bade the guards proclaim to all who waited that any who should be found undeserving would be beaten with stripes.

That edict so frightened the imposters that they quickly fled, and only those few who were actually in want dared to present themselves before the King.

And lo! the task that had seemed too great for one day was performed in a few hours, and when all the needy had been provided for but one of the royal coffers had been opened, and that was scarcely empty!

"What think you, Borland?" asked the Prince, anxiously, "have we done aright?"

"I have learned, Your Majesty," answered the tutor, "that there is a great difference between those who beg and those who suffer for lack of bread. For, while all who needed aid were in truth beggars, not all the beggars needed aid; and hereafter I shall only give alms to those I know to be honestly in want."

"It is wisely said, my friend," returned the Prince, "and I feel I was wrong to doubt the wisdom of my father's councilors. Go, Borland, and ask the King if he will graciously attend me here."

The King arrived and bowed smilingly before the Prince whom he had set to reign in his own place, and at once the boy arose and presented his sire with the scepter and crown, saying,

"Forgive me, oh my King, that I presumed to doubt the wisdom of your rule. For, though the sun has not yet set, I feel that I am all unworthy to sit in your place, and so I willingly resign my power to your more skillful hands. And the coffers which I, in my ignorance, had determined to empty for the benefit of those unworthy, are still nearly full, and more than enough remains for the expenses of the carnival. Therefore forgive me, my father, and let me learn wisdom in the future from the justness of your rule."

Thus ended the reign of Prince Lilimond as King, and not till many years later did he again ascend the throne upon the death of his father.

And really there was not much suffering in the kingdom at any time, as it was a prosperous country and well governed; for, if you look for beggars in any land you will find many, but if you look only for the deserving poor there are less, and these all the more worthy of succor.

I wish all those in power were as kind-hearted as little Prince Lilimond, and as ready to help the needy, for then there would be more light hearts in the world, since it is "better to give than to receive."

Tom, the Piper's Son

Tom, the Piper's Son

Tom, Tom, the piper's son,
Stole a pig and away he run;
The pig was eat and Tom was beat
And Tom ran crying down the street.

Tom, the Piper's Son

THERE was not a worse vagabond in Shrewsbury than old Barney the piper. He never did any work except to play the pipes, and he played so badly that few pennies ever found their way into his pouch. It was whispered around that old Barney was not very honest, but he was so sly and cautious that no one had ever caught him in the act of stealing, although a good many things had been missed after they had fallen into the old man's way.

Barney had one son, named Tom; and they lived all alone in a little hut away at the end of the village street, for Tom's mother had died when he was a baby. You may not suppose that Tom was a very good boy, since he had such a queer father; but neither was he very bad, and the worst fault he had was in obeying his father's wishes when Barney wanted him to steal a chicken for their supper or a pot of potatoes for their breakfast. Tom did not like to steal, but he had no one to teach him to be honest, and so, under his father's guidance, he fell into bad ways.

One morning

> Tom, Tom, the piper's son,
> Was hungry when the day begun;
> He wanted a bun and asked for one,
> But soon found out that there were none.

"What shall we do?" he asked his father.

"Go hungry," replied Barney, "unless you want to take my pipes and play in the village. Perhaps they will give you a penny."

"No," answered Tom, shaking his head; "no one will give me a penny for playing; but Farmer Bowser might give me a penny to stop playing, if I went to his house. He did last week, you know."

"You 'd better try it," said his father; "it 's mighty uncomfortable to be hungry."

So Tom took his father's pipes and walked over the hill to Farmer Bowser's house; for you must know that

> Tom, Tom, the piper's son,
> Learned to play when he was young;
> But the only tune that he could play
> Was "Over the hills and far away."

And he played this one tune as badly as his father himself played, so that the people were annoyed when they heard him, and often begged him to stop.

When he came to Farmer Bowser's house, Tom started up the pipes and began to play with all his

Tom, the Piper's Son

might. The farmer was in his woodshed, sawing wood, so he did not hear the pipes; and the farmer's wife was deaf, and could not hear them. But a little pig that had strayed around in front of the house heard the noise, and ran away in great fear to the pigsty.

Then, as Tom saw the playing did no good, he thought he would sing also, and therefore he began bawling, at the top of his voice,

"Over the hills, not a great ways off,
The woodchuck died with the whooping-cough!"

The farmer had stopped sawing to rest, just then; and when he heard the singing he rushed out of the shed, and chased Tom away with a big stick of wood.

The boy went back to his father, and said, sorrowfully, for he was more hungry than before,

"The farmer gave me nothing but a scolding; but there was a very nice pig running around the yard."

"How big was it?" asked Barney.

"Oh, just about big enough to make a nice dinner for you and me."

The piper slowly shook his head;
"'Tis long since I on pig have fed,
And though I feel it's wrong to steal,
Roast pig is very nice," he said.

Tom knew very well what he meant by that, so he laid down the pipes, and went back to the farmer's house.

When he came near he heard the farmer again sawing wood in the woodshed, and so he went softly up to the pig-sty and reached over and grabbed the little pig by the ears. The pig squealed, of course, but the farmer was making so much noise himself that he did not hear it, and in a minute Tom had the pig tucked under his arm and was running back home with it.

The piper was very glad to see the pig, and said to Tom,

"You are a good son, and the pig is very nice and fat. We shall have a dinner fit for a king."

It was not long before the piper had the pig killed and cut into pieces and boiling in the pot. Only the tail was left out, for Tom wanted to make a whistle of it, and as there was plenty to eat besides the tail his father let him have it.

The piper and his son had a fine dinner that day, and so great was their hunger that the little pig was all eaten up at one meal!

Then Barney lay down to sleep, and Tom sat on a bench outside the door and began to make a whistle out of the pig's tail with his pocket-knife.

Now Farmer Bowser, when he had finished sawing the wood, found it was time to feed the pig, so he took a pail of meal and went to the pigsty. But when he came to the sty there was no pig to be seen, and he searched all round the place for a good hour without finding it.

"Piggy, piggy, piggy!" he called, but no piggy came, and then he knew his pig had been stolen. He was very angry, indeed, for the pig was a great pet, and he had wanted to keep it till it grew very big.

So he put on his coat and buckled a strap around his waist, and went down to the village to see if he could find out who had stolen his pig.

Up and down the street he went, and in and out the lanes, but no traces of the pig could he find anywhere. And that was no great wonder, for the pig was eaten by that time and its bones picked clean.

Finally the farmer came to the end of the street where the piper lived in his little hut, and there he saw Tom sitting on a bench and blowing on a whistle made from a pig's tail.

"Where did you get that tail?" asked the farmer.

"I found it," said naughty Tom, beginning to be frightened.

"Let me see it," demanded the farmer; and when he had looked at it carefully he cried out,

"This tail belonged to my little pig, for I know very well the curl at the end of it! Tell me, you rascal, where is the pig?"

Then Tom fell in a tremble, for he knew his wickedness was discovered.

"The pig is eat, your honor," he answered.

The farmer said never a word, but his face grew black with anger, and, unbuckling the strap that was about his waist, he waved it around his head, and whack! came the strap over Tom's back.

"Ow, ow!" cried the boy, and started to run down the street.

Whack! whack! fell the strap over his shoulders, for the farmer followed at his heels half-way down the street, nor did he spare the strap until he had given Tom a good beating. And Tom was so scared that he never stopped running until he came to the end of the village, and he bawled lustily the whole way and cried out at every step as if the farmer was still at his back.

It was dark before he came back to his home, and his father was still asleep; so Tom crept into the hut and went to bed. But he had received a good lesson, and never after that could the old piper induce him to steal.

When Tom showed by his actions his intention of being honest he soon got a job of work to do, and before long he was able to earn a living more easily, and a great deal more honestly, than when he stole the pig to get a dinner and suffered a severe beating as a punishment.

Tom, Tom, the piper's son
Now with stealing pigs was done,
He'd work all day instead of play,
And dined on tart and currant bun.

Humpty, Dumpty

Humpty Dumpty

Humpty Dumpty sat on a wall,
Humpty Dumpty had a great fall.
  All the King's horses
  And all the King's men
Cannot put Humpty together again.

AT the very top of the hay-mow in the barn, the Speckled Hen had made her nest, and each day for twelve days she had laid in it a pretty white egg. The Speckled Hen had made her nest in this out-of-the-way place so that no one would come to disturb her, as it was her intention to sit upon the eggs until they were hatched into chickens.

Each day, as she laid her eggs, she would cackle to herself, saying, "This will in time be a beautiful chick, with soft, fluffy down all over its body and bright little eyes that will look at the world in amazement. It will be one of my children, and I shall love it dearly."

She named each egg, as she laid it, by the name she should call it when a chick, the first one being "Cluckety-Cluck," and the next "Cadaw-Cut," and so on; and when she came to the twelfth egg she called it "Humpty Dumpty."

This twelfth egg was remarkably big and white and of a very pretty shape, and as the nest was now so full she laid it quite near the edge. And then the Speckled Hen, after looking proudly at her work, went off to the barn-yard, clucking joyfully, in search of something to eat.

When she had gone, Cluckety-Cluck, who was in the middle of the nest and the oldest egg of all, called out, angrily,

"It's getting crowded in this nest; move up there, some of you fellows!" And then he gave Cadaw-Cut, who was above him, a kick.

"I can't move unless the others do; they're crowding me down!" said Cadaw-Cut; and he kicked the egg next above him. And so they continued kicking one another and rolling around in the nest until one kicked Humpty Dumpty, and as he lay on the edge of the nest he was kicked out and rolled down the hay-mow until he came to a stop near the very bottom.

Humpty did not like this very well, but he was a bright egg for one so young, and after he had recovered from his shaking up he began to look about to see where he was. The barn door was open, and he caught a glimpse of trees and hedges, and green grass with a silvery brook running through it. And he saw the waving grain and the tasselled maize and the sunshine flooding it all.

The scene was very enticing to the young egg, and Humpty at once resolved to see something of this great world before going back to the nest.

He began to make his way carefully through the hay, and was getting along fairly well when he heard a voice say,

"Where are you going?"

Humpty looked around and found he was beside a pretty little nest in which was one brown egg.

"Did you speak?" he asked.

"Yes," replied the brown egg; "I asked where you were going."

"Who are you?" enquired Humpty; "do you belong in our nest?"

"Oh, no!" answered the brown egg; "my name is Coutchie-Coulou, and the Black Bantam laid me about an hour ago."

"Oh," said Humpty, proudly; "I belong to the Speckled Hen, myself."

"Do you, indeed!" returned Coutchie-Coulou. "I saw her go by a little while ago, and she 's much bigger than the Black Bantam."

"Yes, and I 'm much bigger than you," replied Humpty. "But I 'm going out to see the world, and if you like to go with me I 'll take good care of you."

"Is n't it dangerous for eggs to go about all by themselves?" asked Coutchie, timidly.

"Perhaps so," answered Humpty; "but it 's dangerous in the nest, too; my brothers might have smashed me with their kicking. However, if we are careful we can't come to much harm; so come along, little one, and I 'll look after you."

Coutchie-Coulou gave him her hand while he helped her out of the nest, and together they crept over the hay until they came to the barn floor. They made for the door at once, holding each other tightly by the hand, and soon came to the threshold, which appeared very high to them.

"We must jump," said Humpty.

"I 'm afraid!" cried Coutchie-Coulou. "And I declare! there 's my mother's voice clucking, and she 's coming this way."

"Then hurry!" said Humpty. "And do not tremble so or you will get yourself all mixed up; it does n't improve eggs to shake them. We will jump, but take care not to bump against me or you may break my shell. Now,—one,—two,—three!"

They held each other's hand and jumped, alighting safely in the roadway. Then, fearing their mothers would see them, Humpty ran as fast as he could go until he and Coutchie were concealed beneath a rose-bush in the garden.

"I 'm afraid we 're bad eggs," gasped Coutchie, who was somewhat out of breath.

"Oh, not at all," replied Humpty; "we were laid only this morning, so we are quite fresh. But now, since we are in the world, we must start out in search of adventure. Here is a roadway beside us which will lead us somewhere or other; so come along, Coutchie-Coulou, and do not be afraid."

The brown egg meekly gave him her hand, and

together they trotted along the roadway until they came to a high stone wall, which had sharp spikes upon its top. It seemed to extend for a great distance, and the eggs stopped and looked at it curiously.

"I'd like to see what is behind that wall," said Humpty, "but I don't think we shall be able to climb over it."

"No, indeed," answered the brown egg, "but just before us I see a little hole in the wall, near the ground; perhaps we can crawl through that."

They ran to the hole and found it was just large enough to admit them. So they squeezed through very carefully, in order not to break themselves, and soon came to the other side.

They were now in a most beautiful garden, with trees and bright-hued flowers in abundance and pretty fountains that shot their merry sprays far into the air. In the center of the garden was a great palace, with bright golden turrets and domes, and many windows that glistened in the sunshine like the sparkle of diamonds.

Richly dressed courtiers and charming ladies strolled through the walks, and before the palace door were a dozen prancing horses, gaily caparisoned, awaiting their riders.

It was a scene brilliant enough to fascinate anyone, and the two eggs stood spellbound while their eyes feasted upon the unusual sight.

"See!" whispered Coutchie-Coulou, "there are

some birds swimming in the water yonder. Let us go and look at them, for we also may be birds some day."

"True," answered Humpty, "but we are just as likely to be omelets or angel's-food. Still, we will have a look at the birds."

So they started to cross the drive on their way to the pond, never noticing that the King and his courtiers had issued from the palace and were now coming down the drive riding upon their prancing steeds. Just as the eggs were in the middle of the drive the horses dashed by, and Humpty, greatly alarmed, ran as fast as he could for the grass.

Then he stopped and looked around, and behold! there was poor Coutchie-Coulou crushed into a shapeless mass by the hoof of one of the horses, and her golden heart was spreading itself slowly over the white gravel of the driveway!

Humpty sat down upon the grass and wept grievously, for the death of his companion was a great blow to him. And while he sobbed, a voice said to him,

"What is the matter, little egg?"

Humpty looked up, and saw a beautiful girl bending over him.

"One of the horses has stepped upon Coutchie-Coulou," he said; "and now she is dead, and I have no friend in all the world."

The girl laughed.

M P
H
D

"Do not grieve," she said, "for eggs are but short-lived creatures at best, and Coutchie-Coulou has at least died an honorable death and saved herself from being fried in a pan or boiled in her own shell. So cheer up, little egg, and I will be your friend—at least so long as you remain fresh. A stale egg I never could abide."

"I was laid only this morning," said Humpty, drying his tears, "so you need have no fear. But do not call me 'little egg,' for I am quite large, as eggs go, and I have a name of my own."

"What is your name?" asked the Princess.

"It is Humpty Dumpty," he answered, proudly. "And now, if you will really be my friend, pray show me about the grounds, and through the palace; and take care I am not crushed."

So the Princess took Humpty in her arms and walked with him all through the grounds, letting him see the fountains and the golden fish that swam in their waters, the beds of lilies and roses, and the pools where the swans floated. Then she took him into the palace, and showed him all the gorgeous rooms, including the King's own bedchamber and the room where stood the great ivory throne.

Humpty sighed with pleasure.

"After this," he said, "I am content to accept any fate that may befall me, for surely no egg before me ever saw so many beautiful sights."

"That is true," answered the Princess; "but now

I have one more sight to show you which will be grander than all the others; for the King will be riding home shortly with all his horses and men at his back, and I will take you to the gates and let you see them pass by."

"Thank you," said Humpty.

So she carried him to the gates, and while they awaited the coming of the King the egg said,

"Put me upon the wall, Princess, for then I shall be able to see much better than in your arms."

"That is a good idea," she answered; "but you must be careful not to fall."

Then she sat the egg gently upon the top of the stone wall, where there was a little hollow; and Humpty was delighted, for from his elevated perch he could see much better than the Princess herself.

"Here they come!" he cried; and, sure enough, the King came riding along the road with many courtiers and soldiers and vassals following in his wake, all mounted upon the finest horses the kingdom could afford.

As they came to the gate and entered at a brisk trot, Humpty, forgetting his dangerous position, leaned eagerly over to look at them. The next instant the Princess heard a sharp crash at her side, and, looking downward, perceived poor Humpty Dumpty, who lay crushed and mangled among the sharp stones where he had fallen!

The Princess sighed, for she had taken quite a

fancy to the egg; but she knew it was impossible to gather it up again or mend the matter in any way, and therefore she returned thoughtfully to the palace.

Now it happened that upon this evening several young men of the kingdom, who were all of high rank, had determined to ask the King for the hand of the Princess; so they assembled in the throne room and demanded that the King choose which of them was most worthy to marry his daughter.

The King was in a quandary, for all the suitors were wealthy and powerful, and he feared that all but the one chosen would become his enemies. Therefore he thought long upon the matter, and at last said,

"Where all are worthy it is difficult to decide which most deserves the hand of the Princess. Therefore I propose to test your wit. The one who shall ask me a riddle I cannot guess, can marry my daughter."

At this the young men looked thoughtful, and began to devise riddles that his Majesty should be unable to guess. But the King was a shrewd monarch, and each one of the riddles presented to him he guessed with ease.

Now there was one amongst the suitors whom the Princess herself favored, as was but natural. He was a slender, fair-haired youth, with dreamy blue eyes and a rosy complexion, and although he loved the Princess dearly he despaired of finding a riddle that the King could not guess.

But while he stood leaning against the wall the Princess approached him and whispered in his ear a riddle she had just thought of. Instantly his face brightened, and when the King called, "Now, Master Gracington, it is your turn," he advanced boldly to the throne.

"Speak your riddle, sir," said the King, gaily; for he thought this youth would also fail, and that he might therefore keep the Princess by his side for a time longer.

But Master Gracington, with downcast eyes, knelt before the throne and spoke in this wise:

"This is my riddle, oh, King:

"Humpty Dumpty sat on a wall,
Humpty Dumpty had a great fall.
All the King's horses
And all the King's men
Cannot put Humpty together again!"

"Read me that, sire, an' you will!"

The King thought earnestly for a long time, and he slapped his head and rubbed his ears and walked the floor in great strides; but guess the riddle he could not.

"You are a humbug, sir!" he cried out at last; "there is no answer to such a riddle."

"You are wrong, sire," answered the young man; "Humpty Dumpty was an egg."

"Why did I not think of that before!" exclaimed

the King; but he gave the Princess to the young man to be his bride, and they lived happily together.

And thus did Humpty Dumpty, even in his death, repay the kindness of the fair girl who had shown him such sights as an egg seldom sees.

The Woman Who
Lived in a Shoe

The Woman Who Lived in a Shoe

There was an old woman
Who lived in a shoe,
She had so many children
She did n't know what to do;
She gave them some broth
Without any bread,
And whipped them all soundly
And sent them to bed.

The Woman Who Lived in a Shoe

A LONG time ago there lived a woman who had four daughters, and these in time grew up and married and went to live in different parts of the country. And the woman, after that, lived all alone, and said to herself, "I have done my duty to the world, and now shall rest quietly for the balance of my life. When one has raised a family of four children and has married them all happily, she is surely entitled to pass her remaining days in peace and comfort."

She lived in a peculiar little house, that looked something like this picture. It was not like most of the houses you see, but the old woman had it built herself, and liked it, and so it did not matter to her how odd it was. It stood upon the top of a little hill, and there was a garden at the back and a pretty green lawn in front, with white gravel paths and many beds of bright colored flowers.

The old woman was very happy and contented there until one day she received a letter saying that her daughter Hannah was dead and had sent her family of five children to their grandmother to be taken care of.

This misfortune ruined all the old woman's dreams of quiet; but the next day the children arrived—three boys and two girls,—and she made the best of it and gave them the beds her own daughters had once occupied, and her own cot as well; and she made a bed for herself on the parlor sofa.

The youngsters were like all other children, and got into mischief once in awhile; but the old woman had much experience with children and managed to keep them in order very well, while they quickly learned to obey her, and generally did as they were bid.

But scarcely had she succedeed in getting them settled in their new home when Margaret, another of her daughters, died, and sent four more children to her mother to be taken care of.

The old woman scarcely knew where to keep this new flock that had come to her fold, for the house was already full; but she thought the matter over and finally decided she must build an addition to her house.

So she hired a carpenter and built what is called a

"lean-to" at the right of her cottage, making it just big enough to accommodate the four new members of her family. When it was completed her house looked very much as it does in this picture.

She put four little cots in her new part of the house, and then she sighed contentedly, and said, "Now all the babies are taken care of and will be comfortable until they grow up." Of course it was much more difficult to manage nine small children than five; and they often led each other into mischief, so that the flower beds began to be trampled upon and the green grass to be worn under the constant tread of little feet, and the furniture to show a good many scratches and bruises.

But the old woman continued to look after them, as well as she was able, until Sarah, her third daughter, also died, and three more children were sent to their grandmother to be brought up.

The old woman was nearly distracted when she heard of this new addition to her family, but she did not give way to despair. She sent for the carpenter again, and had him build another addition to her house, as the picture shows. Then she put three new cots in the new part for the babies to sleep in, and when they arrived

they were just as cozy and comfortable as peas in a pod.

The grandmother was a lively old woman for one of her years, but she found her time now fully occupied in cooking the meals for her twelve small grandchildren, and mending their clothes, and washing their faces, and undressing them at night and dressing them in the morning. There was just a dozen of the babies now, and when you consider they were about the same age you will realize what a large family the old woman had, and how fully her time was occupied in caring for them all.

And now, to make the matter worse, her fourth daughter, who had been named Abigail, suddenly took sick and died, and she also had four small children that must be cared for in some way.

The old woman, having taken the other twelve, could not well refuse to adopt these little orphans also.

"I may as well have sixteen as a dozen," she said, with a sigh; "they will drive me crazy some day, anyhow, so a few more will not matter at all!"

Once more she sent for the carpenter, and bade him build a third addition to the house; and when it was completed she added four more cots to the dozen that were already in use. The house presented a very queer appearance now, but she did not mind that so long as the babies were comfortable. "I shall not have to build again," she said; "and that is one satisfaction. I have now no more daughters to die and leave me their children, and therefore I must make up my mind to do the best I can with the sixteen that have already been inflicted upon me in my old age."

It was not long before all the grass about the house was trodden down, and the white gravel of the walks all thrown at the birds, and the flower beds trampled into shapeless masses by thirty-two little feet that ran about from morn till night. But the old woman did not complain at this; her time was too much taken up with the babies for her to miss the grass and the flowers.

It cost so much money to clothe them that she decided to dress them all alike, so that they looked like the children of a regular orphan asylum. And it cost so much to feed them that she was obliged to give them the plainest food; so there was bread-and-milk for breakfast and milk-and-bread for dinner and bread-and-broth for supper. But it was a good and wholesome diet, and the children thrived and grew fat upon it.

One day a stranger came along the road, and when he saw the old woman's house he began to laugh.

"What are you laughing at, sir?" asked the grandmother, who was sitting upon her door-steps engaged in mending sixteen pairs of stockings.

"At your house," the stranger replied; "it looks for all the world like a big shoe!"

"A shoe!" she said, in surprise.

"Why, yes. The chimneys are shoe-straps, and the steps are the heel, and all those additions make the foot of the shoe."

"Never mind," said the woman; "it may be a shoe, but it is full of babies, and that makes it different from most other shoes."

But the stranger went on to the village and told all he met that he had seen an old woman who lived in a shoe; and soon people came from all parts of the country to look at the queer house, and they usually went away laughing.

The old woman did not mind this at all; she was too busy to be angry. Some of the children were always getting bumped heads or bruised shins, or falling down and hurting themselves, and these had to be comforted. And some were naughty and had to be whipped; and some were dirty and had to be washed; and some were good and had to be kissed. It was "Gran'ma, do this!" and "Gran'ma, do that!" from morning to night, so that the poor grandmother was nearly distracted. The only peace she ever got was when they were all safely tucked in their little cots and were sound asleep; for then, at least, she was free from worry and had a chance to gather her scattered wits.

"There are so many children," she said one day to

the baker-man, "that I often really do n't know what to do!"

"If they were mine, ma'am," he replied, "I'd send them to the poor-house, or else they'd send me to the mad-house."

Some of the children heard him say this, and they resolved to play him a trick in return for his ill-natured speech.

The baker-man came every day to the shoe-house, and brought two great baskets of bread in his arms for the children to eat with their milk and their broth.

So one day, when the old woman had gone to the town to buy shoes, the children all painted their faces, to look as Indians do when they are on the war-path; and they caught the roosters and the turkey-cock and pulled feathers from their tails to stick in their hair. And then the boys made wooden tomahawks for the girls and bows-and-arrows for their own use, and then all sixteen went out and hid in the bushes near the top of the hill.

By and by the baker-man came slowly up the path with a basket of bread on either arm; and just as he reached the bushes there sounded in his ears a most unearthly war-whoop. Then a flight of arrows came from the bushes, and although they were blunt and could do him no harm, they rattled all over his body; and one hit his nose, and another his chin, while several stuck fast in the loaves of bread.

Altogether, the baker-man was terribly frightened;

and when all the sixteen small Indians rushed from the bushes and flourished their tomahawks, he took to his heels and ran down the hill as fast as he could go!

When the grandmother returned she asked,

"Where is the bread for your supper?"

The children looked at one another in surprise, for they had forgotten all about the bread. And then one of them confessed, and told her the whole story of how they had frightened the baker-man for saying he would send them to the poor-house.

"You are sixteen very naughty children!" exclaimed the old woman; "and for punishment you must eat your broth without any bread, and afterwards each one shall have a sound whipping and be sent to bed."

Then all the children began to cry at once, and there was such an uproar that their grandmother had to put cotton in her ears that she might not lose her hearing.

But she kept her promise, and made them eat their broth without any bread; for, indeed, there was no bread to give them.

Then she stood them in a row and undressed them, and as she put the night-dress on each one she gave it a sound whipping and sent it to bed.

They cried some, of course, but they knew very well they deserved the punishment, and it was not long before all of them were sound asleep.

They took care not to play any more tricks on

the baker-man, and as they grew older they were naturally much better behaved.

Before many years the boys were old enough to work for the neighboring farmers, and that made the woman's family a good deal smaller. And then the girls grew up and married, and found homes of their own, so that all the children were in time well provided for.

But not one of them forgot the kind grandmother who had taken such good care of them, and often they tell their children of the days when they lived with the old woman in a shoe and frightened the baker-man almost into fits with their wooden tomahawks.

Little Miss Muffet

Little Miss Muffet

Little Miss Muffet
Sat on a tuffet,
Eating of curds and whey.
There came a great spider
And sat down beside her
And frightened Miss Muffet away.

Little Miss Muffet

LITTLE MISS MUFFET'S father was a big banker in a big city, and he had so much money that the house he lived in was almost as beautiful as a king's palace. It was built of granite and marble, and richly furnished with every luxury that money can buy. There was an army of servants about the house, and many of them had no other duties than to wait upon Miss Muffet, for the little girl was an only child and therefore a personage of great importance. She had a maid to dress her hair and a maid to bathe her, a maid to serve her at table and a maid to tie her shoestrings, and several maids beside. And then there was Nurse Holloweg to look after all the maids and see they did their tasks properly.

The child's father spent his days at his office and his evenings at his club; her mother was a leader in society, and therefore fully engaged from morning till night and from night till morn; so that Little Miss Muffet seldom saw her parents and scarce knew them when she did see them.

I have never known by what name she was christened. Perhaps she did not know herself, for everyone had called her "Miss Muffet" since she could remember. The servants spoke of her respectfully as Miss Muffet. Mrs. Muffet would say, at times, "By the way, Nurse, how is Miss Muffet getting along?" And Mr. Muffet, when he met his little daughter by chance on the walk or in the hallway, would stop and look at her gravely and say, "So this is Miss Muffet. Well, how are you feeling, little one?" And then, without heeding her answer, he would walk away.

Perhaps you think that Miss Muffet, surrounded by every luxury and with a dozen servants to wait upon her, was happy and contented; but such was not the case. She wanted to run and romp, but they told her it was unladylike; she wished to play with other children, but none were rich enough to be proper associates for her; she longed to dig in the dirt in the garden, but Nurse Holloweg was shocked at the very thought. So Miss Muffet became sullen and irritable, and scolded everyone about her, and lived a very unhappy life. And her food was too rich and gave her dyspepsia, so that she grew thin and pale and did not sleep well at night.

One afternoon her mother, who happened to be at

home for an hour, suddenly thought of her little daughter; so she rang the bell and asked for Nurse Holloweg.

"How is Miss Muffet, Nurse?" enquired the lady.

"Very badly, ma'am," was the reply.

"Badly! What do you mean? Is she ill?"

"She 's far from well, ma'am," answered the Nurse, "and seems to be getting worse every day."

"Well," replied the lady; "you must have the doctor to see her; and do n't forget to let me know what he says. That is all, Nurse."

She turned to her novel again, and the Nurse walked away and sent a servant for the doctor. That great man, when he came, shook his head solemnly and said,

"She must have a change. Take her away into the country as soon as possible."

"And very good advice it was, too," remarked the Nurse to one of the maids; "for I feel as if I needed a change myself."

When she reported the matter to Mrs. Muffet the mother answered,

"Very well; I will see Mr. Muffet and have him write out a cheque."

And so it was that a week later Little Miss Muffet went to the country, or rather to a small town where there was a summer hotel that had been highly recommended to Nurse Holloweg; and with her went the string of maids and a wagon-load of boxes and trunks.

The morning after their arrival the little girl asked to go out upon the lawn.

"Well," replied Nurse Holloweg, "Sarah can take you out for half an hour. But remember you are not to run and get heated, for that will ruin your complexion; and you must not speak to any of the common children you meet, for your mother would object; and you must not get your shoes dusty nor your dress soiled, nor disobey Sarah in any way."

Little Miss Muffet went out in a very angry and sulky mood.

"What 's the use of being in the country," she thought, "if I must act just as I did in the city? I hate Nurse Holloweg, and Sarah, and all the rest of them! and if I dared I 'd just—just run away."

Indeed, a few minutes later, when Sarah had fallen asleep upon a bench under a big shade tree, Miss Muffet decided she would really run away for once in her life, and see how it seemed.

There was a pretty lane near by, running between shady trees far out into the country, and, stealing softly away from Sarah's side, the little girl ran as fast as she could go, and never stopped until she was all out of breath.

While she rested and wondered what she could do next, a farmer came along, driving an empty cart.

"I 'll catch on behind," said Miss Muffet, gleefully, "just as I 've seen the boys do in the city. Won't it be fun!"

So she ran and caught on the end of the cart, and actually climbed into it, falling all in a heap upon the straw that lay upon the bottom. But it did n't hurt her at all, and the next minute the farmer whipped up his horses, and they went trotting along the lane, carrying Miss Muffet farther and farther away from hated Nurse Holloweg and the dreadful maids.

She looked around upon the green fields and the waving grain, and drew in deep breaths of the fresh country air, and was happy for almost the first time in her little life. By and by she lay back upon the straw and fell asleep; and the farmer, who did not know she was in his cart, drove on for many miles, until at last he stopped at a small wooden farm-house, and jumped to the ground.

A woman came to the door to greet him, and he said to her,

"Well, mother, we 're home again, you see."

"So I see," she answered; "but did you bring my groceries?"

"Yes," he replied, as he began to unharness the horses; "they are in the cart."

So she came to the cart and looked within, and saw Miss Muffet, who was still asleep.

"Where did you get the little girl?" asked the farmer's wife, in surprise.

"What little girl?" asked he.

"The one in the cart."

He came to the cart and looked in, and was as surprised as his wife.

"She must have climbed into the cart when I left the town," he said; "but waken her, wife, and we will hear what she has to say."

So the farmer's wife shook the girl by the arm, and Miss Muffet sat up in the cart and rubbed her eyes and wondered where she was.

"How came you in my cart?" asked the farmer.

"I caught on behind, and climbed in," answered the girl.

"What is your name, and where do you live?" enquired the farmer's wife.

"My name is Miss Muffet, and I live in a big city, —but where, I do not know."

And that was all she could tell them, so the woman said at last,

"We must keep her till some one comes to claim her, and she can earn her living by helping me make the cheeses."

"That will be nice," said Miss Muffet, with a laugh, "for Nurse Holloweg never lets me do anything, and I should like to help somebody do something."

So they led her into the house, where the farmer's wife wondered at the fine texture of her dress and admired the golden chain that hung around her neck.

"Some one will surely come for her," the woman

said to her husband, "for she is richly dressed and must belong to a family of some importance."

Nevertheless, when they had eaten dinner, for which Little Miss Muffet had a wonderful appetite, the woman took her into the dairy and told her how she could assist her in curdling the milk and preparing it for the cheese-press.

"Why, it's really fun to work," said the girl, at first, "and I should like to live here always. I do hope Nurse Holloweg will not find me."

After a time, however, she grew weary, and wanted to rest; but the woman had not yet finished her cheese-making, so she bade the girl keep at her tasks.

"It's time enough to rest when the work is done," she said, "and if you stay with me you must earn your board. No one is allowed to idle in this house."

So Little Miss Muffet, though she felt like crying and was very tired, kept at her work until at length all was finished and the last cheese was in the press.

"Now," said the farmer's wife, "since you have worked so well I shall give you a dish of curds and whey for your supper, and you may go out into the orchard and eat it under the shade of the trees."

Little Miss Muffet had never eaten curds and whey before, and did not know how they tasted; but she was very hungry, so she took the dish and went into the orchard.

She first looked around for a place to sit down,

and finally discovered a little grassy mound, which is called a tuffet in the country, and seated herself upon it. Then she tasted the curds and whey and found them very good.

But while she was eating she chanced to look down at her feet, and there was a great black spider coming straight towards her. The girl had never seen such an enormous and hideous-looking spider before, and she was so frightened that she gave a scream and tipped backward off the tuffet, spilling the curds and whey all over her dress as she did so. This frightened her more than ever, and as soon as she could get upon her feet she scampered away to the farm-house as fast as she could go, crying bitterly as she ran.

The farmer's wife tried to comfort her, and Miss Muffet, between her sobs, said she had seen "the awfulest, biggest, blackest spider in all the world!"

This made the woman laugh, for she was not afraid of spiders.

Soon after they heard a sound of wheels upon the road and a handsome carriage came dashing up to the gate.

"Has anyone seen a little girl who has run away?" asked Nurse Holloweg, leaning out of the carriage.

"Oh, yes," answered Little Miss Muffet; "here I am, Nurse." And she ran out and jumped into the carriage, for she was very glad to get back again to those who would care for her and not ask her to work making cheeses.

When they were driving back to the town the Nurse said,

"You must promise me, Miss Muffet, never to run away again. You have frightened me nearly into hysterics, and had you been lost your mother would have been quite disappointed."

The little girl was silent for a time; then she answered,

"I will promise not to run away if you will let me play as other children do. But if you do not allow me to run and romp and dig in the ground, I shall keep running away, no matter how many horrid spiders come to frighten me!"

And Nurse Holloweg, who had really been much alarmed at so nearly losing her precious charge, thought it wise to agree to Miss Muffet's terms.

She kept her word, too, and when Little Miss Muffet went back to her home in the city her cheeks were as red as roses and her eyes sparkled with health. And she grew, in time, to be a beautiful young lady, and as healthy and robust as she was beautiful. Seeing which, the doctor put an extra large fee in his bill for advising that the little girl be taken to the country; and Mr. Muffet paid it without a word of protest.

Even after Miss Muffet grew up and was married she never forgot the day that she ran away, nor the curds and whey she ate for her supper, nor the great spider that frightened her away from the tuffet.

Three Wise Men of
Gotham

Three Wise Men of Gotham

Three Wise Men of Gotham
Went to sea in a bowl.
If the bowl had been stronger
My tale had been longer.

THERE lived in the great city of Gotham, over against the north gate, a man who possessed a very wise aspect, but very little else. He was tall and lean, and had a fine large head, bald and smooth upon the top, with a circle of white hair behind the ears. His beard was pure white, and reached to his waist; his eyes were small, dark, and so piercing that they seemed to read your every thought. His eyebrows were very heavy, and as white as his beard. He dressed in a long black mantle with a girdle corded about the middle, and he walked slowly and majestically, and talked no more than he was obliged to.

When this man passed down the street with his stately tread the people all removed their hats and bowed to him with great reverence, saying within themselves,

"He is very wise, this great man; he is a second Socrates."

And soon this was the only name he was called by, and every one in Gotham knew him as "Socrates."

To be sure this man was not really wise. Had they realized the truth, not one he met but knew more than Socrates; but his venerable appearance certainly betokened great wisdom, and no one appeared to remember that things are seldom what they seem.

Socrates would strut about with bowed head and arms clasped behind him, and think:

"My! how wise these people take me to be. Every one admires my beautiful beard. When I look into their faces they drop their eyes. I am, in truth, a wonderful man, and if I say nothing they will believe I am full of wisdom. Ah, here comes the schoolmaster; I shall frown heavily and refuse to notice him, for then he also will be deceived and think I am pondering upon matters of great import."

Really, the one wise thing about this Socrates was his ability to keep quiet. For, saying no word, it was impossible he should betray his ignorance.

Singularly enough, over by the south gate of Gotham there dwelt another wise man, of much the same appearance as Socrates. His white beard was a trifle longer and he had lost his left eye, which was covered by a black patch; but in all other ways his person betokened as much wisdom as that of the other.

He did not walk about, being lazy and preferring

his ease; but he lived in a little cottage with one room, where the people came to consult him in regard to all their troubles.

They had named him Sophocles, and when anything went wrong they would say,

"Let us go and consult Sophocles, for he is very wise and will tell us what to do."

Thus one man, who had sued his neighbor in the courts, became worried over the outcome of the matter and came to consult the wise man.

"Tell me, O Sophocles!" he said, as he dropped a piece of money upon a plate, "shall I win my lawsuit or not?"

Sophocles appeared to ponder for a moment, and then he looked at his questioner with his one eye and replied,

"If it is not decided against you, you will certainly win your suit."

And the man was content, and went away feeling that his money had been well invested.

At another time the mother of a pair of baby twins came to him in great trouble.

"O most wise Sophocles!" she said, "I am in despair! For my little twin girls are just alike, and I have lost the ribbon that I placed on one that I might be able to tell them apart. Therefore I cannot determine which is Amelia and which is Ophelia, and as the priest has christened them by their proper names it would be a sin to call them wrongly."

"Cannot the priest tell?" asked the wise man.

"No one can tell," answered the woman; "neither the priest nor their father nor myself, for they are just alike. And they are yet too young to remember their own names. Therefore your great wisdom is our only resource."

"Bring them to me," commanded Sophocles.

And when they were brought he looked at them attentively and said,

"This is Ophelia and this Amelia. Now tie a red ribbon about Ophelia's wrist and put a blue ribbon on Amelia, and so long as they wear them you will not be troubled to tell them apart."

Everyone marvelled greatly that Sophocles should know the children better than their own mother, but he said to himself,

"Since no no one can prove that I am wrong I am sure to be right;" and thus he maintained his reputation for wisdom.

In a little side street near the center of Gotham lived an old woman named Deborah Smith. Her home was a wretched little hut, for she was poor, and supported herself and her husband by begging in the streets. Her husband was a lazy, short, fat old man, who lay upon a ragged blanket in the hut all day and refused to work.

"One beggar in the family is enough," he used to grumble, when his wife upbraided him, "and I am

Three Wise Men of Gotham

really too tired to work. So let me alone, my Deborah, as I am about to take another nap."

Nothing she could say would arouse him to action, and she finally allowed him to do as he pleased.

But one day she met Socrates walking in the street, and after watching him for a time made up her mind he was nothing more than a fool. Other people certainly thought him wise, but she was a shrewd old woman, and could see well enough that he merely looked wise. The next day she went to the south of the city to beg, and there she heard of Sophocles. When the people repeated his wise sayings she thought

"Here is another fool, for any one could tell as much as this man does."

Still, she went to see Sophocles, and, dropping a penny upon his plate, she asked,

"Tell me, O wise man, how shall I drive my husband to work?"

"By starving him," answered Sophocles; "if you refuse to feed him he must find a way to feed himself."

"That is true," she thought, as she went away; "but any fool could have told me that. This wise man is a fraud; even my husband is as wise as he."

Then she stopped short and slapped her hand against her forehead.

"Why," she cried, "I will make a Wise Man of Perry, my husband, and then he can earn money without working!"

So she went to her husband and said,

"Get up, Perry Smith, and wash yourself; for I am going to make a Wise Man of you."

"I won't," he replied.

"You will," she declared, "for it is the easiest way to earn money I have ever discovered."

Then she took a stick and beat him so fiercely that at last he got up, and agreed to do as she said.

She washed his long beard until it was as white as snow, and she shaved his head to make him look bald and venerable. Then she brought him a flowing black robe with a girdle at the middle; and when he was dressed, lo! he looked fully as wise as either Socrates or Sophocles.

"You must have a new name," she said, "for no one will ever believe that Perry Smith is a Wise Man. So I shall hereafter call you Pericles, the Wisest Man of Gotham!"

She then led him into the streets, and to all they met she declared,

"This is Pericles, the wisest man in the world."

"What does he know?" they asked.

"Everything, and much else," she replied.

Then came a carter, and putting a piece of money in the hand of Pericles, he enquired,

"Pray tell me of your wisdom what is wrong with my mare?"

"How should I know?" asked Pericles.

"I thought you knew everything," returned the carter, in surprise.

"I do," declared Pericles; "but you have not told me what her symptoms are."

"She refuses to eat anything," said the carter.

"Then she is not hungry," returned Pericles; "for neither man nor beast will refuse to eat when hungry."

And the people who heard him whispered together and said,

"Surely this is a wise man, for he has told the carter what is wrong with his mare."

After a few days the fame of Pericles' sayings came to the ears of both Socrates and Sophocles, and they resolved to see him, for each feared he would prove more wise than they were, knowing themselves to be arrant humbugs. So one morning the three wise men met together outside the hut of Pericles, and they sat themselves down upon stools, facing each other, while a great crowd of people gathered around to hear the words of wisdom that dropped from their lips.

But for a time all three were silent, and regarded one another anxiously, for each feared he might betray himself.

Finally Sophocles winked his one eye at the others and said, in a grave voice,

"The earth is flat; for, were it round, as some fools say, all the people would slide off the surface."

Then the people, who had listened eagerly, clapped their hands together and murmured,

"Sophocles is wisest of all. What he says is truth."

This provoked Socrates greatly, for he felt his reputation was in danger; so he said with a frown,

"The world is shallow, like a dish; were it flat the water would all run over the edges, and we should have no oceans."

Then the people applauded more loudly than before, and cried,

"Socrates is right! he is wisest of all."

Pericles, at this, shifted uneasily upon his stool, for he knew he must dispute the matter boldly or his fame would depart from him. Therefore he said, with grave deliberation,

"You are wrong, my friends. The world is hollow, like the shell of a cocoanut, and we are all inside the shell. The sky above us is the roof, and if you go out upon the ocean you will come to a place, no matter in which direction you go, where the sky and the water meet. I know this is true, for I have been to sea."

The people cheered loudly at this, and said,

"Long live Pericles, the wisest of the wise men!"

"I shall hold I am right," protested Sophocles, "until Pericles and Socrates prove that I am wrong."

"That is fair enough," said the people.

"And I also shall hold myself to be right until they prove me wrong," declared Socrates, firmly.

"I know I am right," said Pericles, "for you cannot prove me wrong."

"We can take a boat and sail over the sea," remarked Socrates, "and when we come to the edge we will know the truth. Will you go?"

"Yes," answered Sophocles; and Pericles, because he did not dare refuse, said "Yes" also.

Then they went to the shore of the sea, and the people followed them. There was no boat to be found anywhere, for the fishers were all away upon the water; but there was a big wooden bowl lying upon the shore, which the fishermen used to carry their fish to market in.

"This will do," said Pericles, who, because he weighed the most, was the greatest fool of the three.

So the wise men all sat within the bowl, with their feet together, and the people pushed them out into the water.

The tide caught the bowl and floated it out to sea, and before long the wise men were beyond sight of land.

They were all greatly frightened, for the bowl was old and cracked, and the water leaked slowly through until their feet were covered. They clung to the edge with their hands and looked at one another with white faces. Said Pericles,

"I was a fool to come to sea in this bowl."

"Ah," remarked Socrates, "if you are a fool, as you confess, then you cannot be a wise man."

"No," answered Pericles, "but I 'll soon be a dead man."

"I also was a fool," said Sophocles, who was weeping from his one eye and trembling all over, "for if I had stayed upon land I would not have been drowned."

"Since you both acknowledge it," sighed Socrates, "I will confess that I also am a fool, and have always been one; but I looked so wise the people insisted I must know everything!"

"Yes, yes," Sophocles groaned, "the people have murdered us!"

"My only regret," said Pericles, "is that my wife is not with me. If only she were here"—

He did not finish what he was saying, for just then the bowl broke in two. And the people are still waiting for the three wise men to come back to them.

Little Bun Rabbit

Little Bun Rabbit

"Oh, Little Bun Rabbit, so soft and so shy,
Say, what do you see with your big, round eye?"
"On Christmas we rabbits," says Bunny so shy,
"Keep watch to see Santa go galloping by."

LITTLE Dorothy had passed all the few years of her life in the country, and being the only child upon the farm she was allowed to roam about the meadows and woods as she pleased. On the bright summer mornings Dorothy's mother would tie a sun-bonnet under the girl's chin, and then she romped away to the fields to amuse herself in her own way.

She came to know every flower that grew, and to call them by name, and she always stepped very carefully to avoid treading on them, for Dorothy was a kind-hearted child and did not like to crush the pretty flowers that bloomed in her path. And she was also very fond of all the animals, and learned to know them well, and even to understand their language, which very few people can do. And the animals loved Dorothy in turn, for the word passed around amongst them that she could be trusted to do them no harm. For the horse, whose soft nose

Dorothy often gently stroked, told the cow of her kindness, and the cow told the dog, and the dog told the cat, and the cat told her black kitten, and the black kitten told the rabbit when one day they met in the turnip patch.

Therefore when the rabbit, which is the most timid of all animals and the most difficult to get acquainted with, looked out of a small bush at the edge of the wood one day and saw Dorothy standing a little way off, he did not scamper away, as is his custom, but sat very still and met the gaze of her sweet eyes boldly, although perhaps his heart beat a little faster than usual.

Dorothy herself was afraid she might frighten him away, so she kept very quiet for a time, leaning silently against a tree and smiling encouragement at her timorous companion until the rabbit became reassured and blinked his big eyes at her thoughtfully. For he was as much interested in the little girl as she in him, since it was the first time he had dared to meet a person face to face.

Finally Dorothy ventured to speak, so she asked, very softly and slowly,

"Oh, Little Bun Rabbit, so soft and so shy,
Say, what do you see with your big, round eye?"

"Many things," answered the rabbit, who was pleased to hear the girl speak in his own language; "in summer-time I see the clover-leaves that I love to feed upon and the cabbages at the end of the farmer's garden. I see the cool bushes where I can hide from my enemies, and I see the dogs and the men long before they can see me, or know that I am near, and therefore I am able to keep out of their way."

"Is that the reason your eyes are so big?" asked Dorothy.

"I suppose so," returned the rabbit; "you see we have only our eyes and our ears and our legs to defend ourselves with. We cannot fight, but we can always run away, and that is a much better way to save our lives than by fighting."

"Where is your home, bunny?" enquired the girl.

"I live in the ground, far down in a cool, pleasant hole I have dug in the midst of the forest. At the bottom of the hole is the nicest little room you can imagine, and there I have made a soft bed to rest in at night. When I meet an enemy I run to my hole and jump in, and there I stay until all danger is over."

"You have told me what you see in summer," continued Dorothy, who was greatly interested in the rabbit's account of himself, "but what do you see in the winter?"

"In winter we rabbits," said Bunny so shy,
"Keep watch to see Santa go galloping by."

"And do you ever see him?" asked the girl, eagerly.

"Oh, yes; every winter. I am not afraid of him, nor of his reindeer. And it is such fun to see him come dashing along, cracking his whip and calling out cheerily to his reindeer, who are able to run even swifter than we rabbits. And Santa Claus, when he sees me, always gives me a nod and a smile, and then I look after him and his big load of toys which he is carrying to the children, until he has galloped away out of sight. I like to see the toys, for they are so bright and pretty, and every year there is something new amongst them. Once I visited Santa, and saw him make the toys."

"Oh, tell me about it!" pleaded Dorothy.

"It was one morning after Christmas," said the rabbit, who seemed to enjoy talking, now that he had overcome his fear of Dorothy, "and I was sitting by the road-side when Santa Claus came riding back in his empty sleigh. He does not come home quite so fast as he goes, and when he saw me he stopped for a word.

"'You look very pretty this morning, Bun Rabbit,' he said, in his jolly way; 'I think the babies would love to have you to play with.'

"'I do n't doubt it, your honor,' I answered; 'but they 'd soon kill me with handling, even if they did not scare me to death; for babies are very rough with their playthings.'

"'That is true,' replied Santa Claus; 'and yet you are so soft and pretty it is a pity the babies can't have you. Still, as they would abuse a live rabbit I think I shall make them some toy rabbits, which they cannot hurt; so if you will jump into my sleigh with me and ride home to my castle for a few days, I 'll see if I can't make some toy rabbits just like you.'

"Of course I consented, for we all like to please old Santa, and a minute later I had jumped into the sleigh beside him and we were dashing away at full speed toward his castle. I enjoyed the ride very much, but I enjoyed the castle far more; for it was one of the loveliest places you could imagine. It stood on the top of a high mountain and is built of gold and silver bricks, and the windows are pure diamond crystals. The rooms are big and high, and there is a soft carpet upon every floor and many strange things scattered around to amuse one. Santa Claus lives there all alone, except for old Mother Hubbard, who cooks the meals for him; and her cupboard is never bare now, I can promise you! At the top of the castle there is one big room, and that is Santa's work-shop, where he makes the toys. On one side is his work-bench, with plenty of saws and hammers and jack-knives; and on another side is the paint-bench, with paints of every color and brushes of every size and shape. And in other places are great shelves, where the toys are put to dry and keep new and bright until Christmas comes and it is time to load them all into his sleigh.

"After Mother Hubbard had given me a good

dinner, and I had eaten some of the most delicious clover I have ever tasted, Santa took me up into his work-room and sat me upon the table.

"'If I can only make rabbits half as nice as you are,' he said, 'the little ones will be delighted.' Then he lit a big pipe and began to smoke, and soon he took a roll of soft fur from a shelf in a corner and commenced to cut it out in the shape of a rabbit. He smoked and whistled all the time he was working, and he talked to me in such a jolly way that I sat perfectly still and allowed him to measure my ears and my legs so that he could cut the fur into the proper form.

"'Why, I 've got your nose too long, Bunny,' he said once; and so he snipped a little off the fur he was cutting, so that the toy rabbit's nose should be like mine. And again he said, 'Good gracious! the ears are too short entirely!' So he had to get a needle and thread and sew on more fur to the ears, so that they might be the right size. But after a time it was all finished, and then he stuffed the fur full of sawdust and sewed it up neatly; after which he put in some glass eyes that made the toy rabbit look wonderfully life-like. When it was all done he put it on the table beside me, and at first I did n't know whether I was the live rabbit or the toy rabbit, we were so much alike.

"'It 's a very good job,' said Santa, nodding his head at us pleasantly; 'and I shall have to make a lot of these rabbits, for the little children are sure to be greatly pleased with them.'

"So he immediately began to make another, and this time he cut the fur just the right size, so that it was even better than the first rabbit.

"'I must put a squeak in it,' said Santa.

"So he took a box of squeaks from a shelf and put one into the rabbit before he sewed it up. When it was all finished he pressed the toy rabbit with his thumb, and it squeaked so naturally that I jumped off the table, fearing at first the new rabbit was alive. Old Santa laughed merrily at this, and I soon recovered from my fright and was pleased to think the babies were to have such pretty playthings.

"'After this,' said Santa Claus, 'I can make rabbits without having you for a pattern; but if you like you may stay a few days longer in my castle and amuse yourself.'

"I thanked him and decided to stay. So for several days I watched him making all kinds of toys, and I wondered to see how quickly he made them, and how many new things he invented.

"'I almost wish I was a child,' I said to him one day, 'for then I too could have playthings.'

"'Ah, you can run about all day, in summer and in winter, and enjoy yourself in your own way,' said Santa; 'but the poor little children are obliged to stay in the house in the winter and on rainy days in the summer, and then they must have toys to amuse them and keep them contented.'

"I knew this was true, so I only said, admiringly,

"'You must be the quickest and the best workman in all the world, Santa.'

"'I suppose I am,' he answered; 'but then, you see, I have been making toys for hundreds of years, and I make so many it is no wonder I am skillful. And now, if you are ready to go home, I'll hitch up the reindeer and take you back again.'

"'Oh, no,' said I, 'I prefer to run by myself, for I can easily find the way and I want to see the country.'

"'If that is the case,' replied Santa, 'I must give you a magic collar to wear, so that you will come to no harm.'

"So, after Mother Hubbard had given me a good meal of turnips and sliced cabbage, Santa Claus put the magic collar around my neck and I started for home. I took my time on the journey, for I knew nothing could harm me, and I saw a good many strange sights before I got back to this place again."

"But what became of the magic collar?" asked Dorothy, who had listened with breathless interest to the rabbit's story.

"After I got home," replied the rabbit, "the collar disappeared from around my neck, and I knew Santa had called it back to himself again. He did not give it to me, you see; he merely let me take it on my journey to protect me. The next Christmas, when I watched by the road-side to see Santa, I was pleased to notice a great many of the toy rabbits sticking out of the loaded sleigh. The babies must have liked them, too, for every year since I have seen them amongst the toys.

"Santa never forgets me, and every time he passes he calls out, in his jolly voice,

"'A merry Christmas to you, Bun Rabbit! The babies still love you dearly.'"

The Rabbit paused, and Dorothy was just about to ask another question when Bunny raised his head and seemed to hear something coming.

"What is it?" enquired the girl.

"It's the farmer's big shepherd dog," answered the Rabbit, "and I must be going before he sees me, or I shall shall have to run for my life. So good bye, Dorothy; I hope we shall meet again, and then I will gladly tell you more of my adventures."

The next instant he had sprung into the wood, and all that Dorothy could see of him was a gray streak darting in and out amongst the trees.